THE WINNER'S CIRCLE

GOLDEN FILLY SERIES

THE WINNER'S CIRCLE

LAURAINE SNELLING

BETHANY HOUSE PUBLISHERS
MINNEAPOLIS, MINNESOTA 55438

Cover by John Schreiner

Published by Bethany House Publishers
A Ministry of Bethany Fellowship, Inc.
11300 Hampshire Avenue South
Minneapolis, Minnesota 55438

Printed in the United States of America.

Library of Congress Cataloging-in-Publication Data

Snelling, Lauraine.
    The winner's circle / Lauraine Snelling.
       p. cm. — (The golden filly series ; bk.10)
    Summary: As she and her filly Firefly recover from a tragic racing accident, Trish tries to find out who is behind the disturbing threats she continues to receive and she discovers that God has a perfect plan for her life.

    [1. Horse racing—Fiction. 2. Christian life—Fiction.]
I. Title. II. Series: Snelling, Lauraine. Golden Filly series ; bk.10.
PZ7.S677Wi   1994
[Fic]—dc20   94–49227
ISBN 1–55661–533–7   CIP
                                             AC

To Wayne,
my best friend
and the love of my life.
We have plenty of adventures
yet to come.

LAURAINE SNELLING is a full-time writer who has authored a number of books, both fiction and non-fiction, as well as written articles for a wide range of magazines and weekly features for local newspapers. She also teaches writing courses and trains people in speaking skills. She and her husband, Wayne, have two grown children and make their home in California.

Her lifelong love of horses began at age five with a pony named Polly and continued with Silver, Kit, Rowdy, and her daughter's horse, Cimeron, which starred in her first children's book, *Tragedy on the Toutle*.

CHAPTER ONE

What about Firefly? Trish Evanston sluggishly swam away from the nightmare and back to consciousness. But it wasn't just a bad dream. The horrifying accident at the track had really happened.

"Trish, Tee, it's okay." The comforting sound of her mother's voice brought Trish instantly and totally awake.

"No, it's not. Have you been over to see Firefly?" Trish scrubbed the palms of her hands across her eyes and at the same moment ducked away from the pain. All the moving parts of her body were connected, in one way or another, to her broken ribs—and the incision to repair her punctured lung. The accident at the track hadn't been kind to either her or the filly.

"I've got to get over to the vet's to see her."

"Not until the doctor agrees." Marge folded her arms across her chest, a sure sign she didn't plan on changing her mind.

Hospitals were not Trish's favorite place to be, let alone hospital beds. Tricia Marie Evanston, as her mother called her when peeved beyond measure (which had happened with increasing frequency the last two days), begged the doctor for the third time to release her.

"Ah'm sorry, ma deah," he repeated for the third time in his smooth southern drawl. "Y'all just need some more healin' time here. Punctured lungs don't heal overnight."

By now Trish was fed up to her ears with soft-spoken southerners who smiled so winningly and did what they thought best anyway. All she wanted was out.

"But, Mother, what are they going to do about Firefly?" Trish clenched the blanket in her fists.

"They're doing what they can." Marge, slumped in the orange plastic chair beside the bed, studied her cuticles.

"How bad is it?"

Marge shook her head, obviously wishing she were anywhere but under Trish's grilling. "Infection has set in; she's not eating and drinking well. They've called in more equine specialists. Donald Shipson has been taking care of her so I could be here with you."

"I know and I'm sorry to be such a grouch." Trish ignored the pang of guilt. She tried to catch her mother's gaze, but Marge refused. *She's not telling me everything.* The thought clenched in her stomach. But rather than attacking, Trish continued her pleading. "But I'm fine now. Why won't they let me out of here?"

"Maybe the doctor figures you'll do something stupid."

Trish attempted an innocent look and failed miserably. "Me? What could I do? I can hardly even walk down the hall without puffing." She didn't add, *and hurting.* The doctor had told her that ribs smashed like hers would be painful, but pain didn't begin to cover it. She turned to stare out the window of her private room in Louisville Memorial Hospital. The Ohio River flowed serenely toward its distant rendezvous with the mighty Mississippi. "I've been cooped up in here nearly a week."

"The first three days you were too sick to care, but who's counting?"

Trish was. She couldn't let go of the terrifying feeling. "Mother?" She chose her words with great care. "Please answer me honestly. What more do you know about Firefly?"

"Nothing, nothing at all. You'll be able to see for yourself as soon as you're well enough."

Mother wouldn't lie to me, would she?

"Mail call." The bubbly day-nurse, Sue Morgan, interrupted their discussion. She hefted a shoe box full of letters and cards. "We're weighing the mail now rather than counting. This one's about two and a half pounds."

"Good grief." Marge and Trish just looked at each other and shook their heads.

"Where do you want this?" The nurse glanced around the room. Flowers and plants hid every inch of flat surface, and cards and posters covered half the walls. Balloons—square, round, and every color of the rainbow—bobbed in the air currents in the corner designated as "the balloon corral."

Trish shrugged. "Over by the wall, I guess. How am I ever gonna answer all these cards?"

"Ask some of your friends to help you when you get home." The nurse tossed a couple of extra large envelopes—one hot pink, the other neon green—on the bed. "These didn't fit in the box. Guess you can start there." She headed for the door and turned to ask, "Can I get you anything? Ice, water, ice cream, tapioca, or chocolate pudding?" She ticked them off on her fingers, her eyes twinkling above cheeks always rounded by a grin. "A Diet Coke?"

"Oh, yes please. That sounds heavenly."

"Which?"

"All of the above. If I keep eating like this I'll be fat as a pig before they let me out of here."

"We don't intend to keep you forever, you know. Just seems like it." She flashed Trish another grin, the kind that did good things for anyone in sight. "Marge, you want something too?"

"No thanks." Marge checked her watch. "I should go back to the motel and get a shower."

"Shower . . . that's it. I get to wash my hair today. You promised." Trish ran her fingers through hair that felt as grimy as a horse's tail after a muddy race.

"I was hoping you'd forget. It doesn't look so bad when you keep it braided like that."

"Yeah right." Trish's look accused the young woman of lying through her teeth.

Sue leaned one hand against the doorjamb. "You feel up to bending over the sink? Doc says to keep that incision dry for a couple more days. Then we can plastic-tape you."

"Anything. Red's coming tonight."

"So what's new? I hear that good-lookin' redhead shows up here every night."

Trish raised her voice to talk over the nurse's comment. "And I want to look human again."

Sue winked at Marge. "Sure wish he'd come earlier so's I could meet him. Or maybe he could bring a friend."

"He's up in the eighth today. Sorry." Trish felt a grin sneak up from inside and blossom on her face. How come she could never think of or talk about this guy without a smile and the warm squigglies down in her middle that went along with it?

"Speaking of hair washing." Marge fluffed the gray-streaked sides of her hair with her fingertips. "Mine could do with some attention so I'll let you two play beauty parlor while I do the same for me."

"There's a good beauty shop right around the corner if you like. I know getting my hair done makes me feel like a whole new woman." Sue headed for the door. "I'll call and make you an appointment right now."

"That sounds wonderful." Marge looked back to her daughter. "You're sure you don't need me?"

"Hey, I'm seventeen years old, remember? Time for me to stand on my own feet." Trish made a gesture that took in the hospital bed and her body in it. "Or at least, as soon as they let me."

"Good news." Sue returned in a rush. "They can take you in fifteen minutes. Turn right out the front entrance and left at the corner. You'll see it—Emma Lou's Emporium—two doors down." She handed Trish a cardboard container of orange and vanilla ice cream and set a can of Diet Coke next to a glass of ice. "Soon's you finish this, we'll get you to the bathroom."

Marge dropped a kiss on the top of Trish's head and made a face. "Yuk, you smell like . . ."

"Bye, Mom, and thanks a million. You really know how to make a sick daughter feel good." Trish dug into the ice cream and licked her spoon. She waved as Marge left.

Her mom really did need some time off. Ever since the surgery, her mother had been there every time Trish had opened her eyes—even during the long nights when the pain outlasted the medication. Last night had been the first time Marge had slept somewhere other than in a foldout chair by Trish's bedside.

Trish eyed the new box of mail waiting for her against the wall. So far there had been no cards or cut-out notes from "The Jerk," as they all called whoever had been harassing her. The police had taken the threats seriously enough to assign her a bodyguard. Officer Amy Jones had accompanied Trish from Runnin' On Farm in Vancouver, Washington, and returned to Portland while Trish was still in intensive care.

Trish ate her ice cream on autopilot, her gaze focused on the box. *I should go over and see if there really are any envelopes with no return, a block-printed address, and a Portland cancellation.*

I really should. Instead she poured her drink into the glass and watched it foam. Just the thought of The Jerk brought back the dry throat and pounding heart she felt when she had opened the card that said "I'll get you." Letting that thought in was like opening a crate of snakes. Other thoughts slithered out.

What was happening with Firefly? What was her mother leaving out? Had they caught The Jerk yet? Who could it be? She poked the fears back in the box and slammed the lid. *Concentrate on the ice cream,* she told herself. *That's safer.*

She ate the remaining bites of ice cream before flipping back the covers and dangling her legs over the side of the bed. Maybe she should study for a while first. She glared at the stack of books on her bed stand. History, English, government. She shook her head. Later.

Once on her feet she crossed the room to the balloon corral and tapped the shocking pink one in front. That set all the others to bobbing. People she'd never heard of had sent her balloons, just to make her feel better.

One really pretty arrangement of pink rosebuds had arrived the day before—from Amy and Officer Parks. Trish sniffed the opening buds and reread the card. It didn't mention if they'd heard from The Jerk either. It just said they were praying for her to get well quick.

Trish felt a warm glow around her heart. Amy admitted that seeing the Evanstons' faith in action made her want the same. And now she wrote that she was praying for Trish. *Dad, you were right,* Trish thought. *It's walkin' the walk, not just talkin' the talk that brings people to Jesus.*

Trish picked up a fluffy white teddy bear and cuddled it in both arms. "Hug this fellow and think of me," its name tag said, signed "Red." She rested her chin on top of the bear's head and eyed the box on the floor. Where had all her guts gone—to be so spooked by a box of cards?

"Must have left them on the operating table," she whispered into the bear's ear. She took in as deep a breath as her ribs would allow without making her flinch, set the bear back down on the end of the bed, and squatted down to pick up the box.

"What are you doing down there?" Sue crossed the room to stand by Trish's side.

"Going to look for ah—any . . ." Trish swallowed her words and changed directions. She rose to her feet, relief making her grin. "Can we do my hair now?" Why tell Sue about the messages she'd received? Maybe it was all over by now anyway.

————

By the time Sue had finished washing and towel-drying her patient's hair, Trish felt as if she'd run a marathon. Leaning over the sink made her woozy from the pain, but she toughed it out. Clean hair was worth whatever she had to go through to get it.

"Think you can dry it?" Sue handed Trish the blow-dryer and plugged it into the outlet at the head of the bed.

"Sure, why not?" Trish turned the machine on and raised her arms to begin the process. "Ow!" She let her arms fall back on the bed.

"That's why. An incision and broken ribs make for sore muscles. You just wait a bit. After I take care of the lady next door, I'll be back."

For once Trish didn't argue. Where would she go? She didn't dare draw a deep breath either for fear of another pain attack. She leaned her head back and concentrated on relaxing. The pain-caused wobblies left and she opened her eyes, eying the hair dryer as if it might bite her. She hated to admit the doctor might have been right. But if she didn't get going soon, Firefly could get worse.

"Father, what am I to do?" She listened for an answer to her whispered prayer, but nothing came. Really, what could she do? She could hear her mother's voice: *"Just behave yourself and do what the doctor says. Bad thoughts can't help you feel better faster but good thoughts can."* Sometimes her mother sounded just like her father had before he died from cancer a few months before.

Sue popped her head in the doorway. "Just one more sec." And popped it back out. Trish could hear the nurse's heels squeeching away down the hall.

You could study, you know. Nagger, as she called her resident inner critic, seemed to whisper in her ear. *It would make the time go faster.*

"There now," Sue said after blow drying Trish's hair, "you look stunning. And about ready for a nap." She patted Trish on the shoulder. "See you tomorrow unless they let you bust out of here before then."

"Thanks." Trish climbed back in bed. "You've been super."

Sue gave her patient a gentle hug. "So have you, kid. Take care of yourself."

––––––––

Trish had finished her dinner and was watching television when she heard a familiar voice in the hall. Quickly she smoothed her hair back, tucking the right side behind her ear and fluffing her bangs. She should have put on some lip gloss. She started to raise the lid on her tray table to see the mirror, but it was too late.

Red's deep chuckle, the kind no one could resist, preceded him into the room.

"Don't make me laugh!" Trish warned him with a raised hand, as if she could stop him like cops halt traffic.

"Is that any way to greet a beat-up jockey?" Red paused in the door, the same height as Trish at five feet four and slender, but with powerful shoulders. His blue eyes sparkled like sun dancing on the Pacific and matched the blue sling holding his left arm against his body.

"What happened?"

"I did a Trish Evanston. You know, take a header and your horse down with you." He shrugged his shoulders and flinched at the motion. "But I roll better'n you do."

"Are you broken anywhere?"

"Naaa, just popped out the joint. Had to agree to the sling or the old battle-ax wouldn't let me out of the infirmary." Red stood by the side of the bed and touched Trish's cheek with a gentle finger. His voice softened. "You're looking much better."

Trish felt her insides melt and puddle in her middle. She swallowed. Her cheek still flamed from his touch.

"Ah . . ." She wanted to say something. Where was her brain? Down in the mush in her middle?

"Ah . . ." She cleared her throat. When he bent down to kiss her, words weren't necessary anyway. Her eyelids drifted shut as his lips feathered over hers. Things were definitely looking up.

He straightened. His Adam's apple bobbed. She swallowed a grin.

From the television set hanging on the wall above him, she caught a line about horse racing. "Just a minute." She picked up the remote and clicked the volume higher. Red turned to watch with her. A sportscaster's serious face filled the screen.

"Here's a late report on Trish Evanston, the Triple-Crown-winning female jockey who was injured at Churchill Downs on Saturday.

"While Trish is recovering at Louisville Memorial, her filly Firefly is being cared for at the Garden Grove Veterinary Hospital. According to the reports we have received from Doctor Grant, head of surgery there, they may have to put the horse down."

CHAPTER TWO

Trish clamped her teeth on her bottom lip to keep from screaming. "No! They can't put her down. Not Firefly." Her gaze swung from the screen to Red's tortured face. "You knew! And you didn't tell me. Mom didn't either. If I can't trust you guys to tell me the truth, I'll have to go see for myself."

"No, Trish, listen!" Red shook his head, trying to interrupt her. "Your mother doesn't know any more about this than I do. Unless Firefly's failed in the last hour, the reporters are exaggerating, as usual. You know what they're like."

"I'm listening." Trish couldn't force her voice above a whisper. "So tell me, how is she? Really!"

Red shifted from one foot to the other. "Well, they have her on massive antibiotics to fight the infection." He stared into Trish's eyes, pleading for her to believe him.

"I know." Trish wanted to squeeze the words out of him but was afraid to. Next to Spitfire, Firefly was her favorite horse. And also her father's. Sired by Seattle Slew, the same stallion who sired Spitfire, Firefly would be valuable as a broodmare even if she could never race again. "She's too fine a horse to be put down. She's a

17

fighter! I know she can make it." Trish wasn't sure who she was trying to convince, Red or herself. She slammed her fists into the bedcovers. "I've got to get out of here."

"You couldn't do any more than they're already doing."

The comment brought her up short. What *could* she do? "Is she eating?"

Red shook his head.

"Drinking?"

"A little." He studied the toe of his boots. "They have her on IV's."

"I could help. I know I could." Trish's runaway thoughts screamed so loud she was sure everyone in the hospital could hear them. "She's my horse. They can't put her down without my consent." Another thought caught her on the jaw. "Or could my mother give the okay?" *She wouldn't do that to me, would she?* The thought hurt as much as her ribs.

Red turned, relief evident in the smile he gave the entering doctor.

"Good evenin', y'all. Sorry ah'm so late, but ah have good news for you, Trish. You can be released in the mahnin', soon's we remove that drain and finish the paper work."

"In the morning? Why not tonight?" Trish knew her tone lacked any trace of gratitude, but she couldn't help it.

The doctor shook his head and peered at her over his half glasses. "Child, child, so impatient." His sparkling blue eyes and easy smile removed any sting from his words. "Now, where is your mother? She'll have to sign the forms."

"She went down for dinner." Trish grimaced when

she crossed her arms over her chest, then tried to cover up the reflex.

"Those ribs will hurt for some time yet. You have to take it easy for a few weeks, you hear me?" He tapped his pencil on the edge of her chart holder.

Trish nodded. What did he think she was going to do—go out and ride in tomorrow's program?

You probably would if you had a mount. Nagger seemed to be sitting on the pillow, right beside her ear. *And sulking never gets you anywhere. You aren't very good at it.*

Trish shot a look at Red and caught the glint of laughter in his eyes. What was he, another mind reader? She pulled her manners out from wherever they'd been hiding and graciously thanked the doctor for his good news.

"Tell your mother I'll talk with her in the morning. I'll be here right around eight." He stopped at the door. "I sure hope to see you racing at Churchill Downs next year, young lady. From all I hear, you have a great future ahead of you."

"Funny he should say that," Trish said after he left.

"Not really. Everyone in Louisville keeps track of horse racing. It's our claim to fame. He probably watched you win the Derby last spring." Red stared around the room at all her gifts. "What are you going to do with all this stuff?"

"Pack it, I guess." Trish let her gaze wander from the flowers to the stuffed animals to the balloons bobbing in the corral. An idea exploded in her head. "I could take some of this to the children's cancer floor. Maybe the toys would make them feel better."

"Make who feel better?" Marge paused at the door in

time to watch her daughter bail out of bed as fast as her bruised and broken body allowed.

"The kids who are here for chemotherapy treatments or whatever." Trish checked the stuffed gorilla in the corner. Sure enough, her organized mother had the card pinned to the animal's ribbon. The name of whoever had sent it was written on the card. She looked at her mother and shook her head. "You're something else, Mom."

"What did I do now?" Marge wore the familiar confused look that dealing with her daughter in full gallop caused. "You might bring me up to speed here."

"I get out of here in the morning, and we're taking some of this stuff up to the kids on the pediatric ward to cheer them up." Trish gathered all the balloon strings and tied them together with one string. "How about asking the nurse if we can have a cart or something?"

Trish moved at half speed. Bending over was *not* her best move. And lifting anything, even a floppy-eared bunny with blue print overalls, gave her pause. But when she reached up to take down a poster of Garfield scarfing down an entire chocolate cake, she couldn't stifle the groan.

"Okay, that's it." Marge took Trish's arm and eased her back to the bed. "You sit. We'll work."

For once in her life Trish didn't feel like arguing.

———

Later that night, Trish let the tears flow. The kids had loved the gifts. They'd laughed and thanked Trish, squeezing the stuffed animals as if someone might snatch them away. And that was the problem. Seeing the children hooked up to IV's—and one little boy barfing because of the chemotherapy—brought back the memories of her father's illness. Like those kids, he had smiled and made jokes when he could.

Trish hugged her ribs, stifling her sobs to sniffles and teary eyes.

"Can I get you anything, Trish?" Silent as a shadow, the evening nurse appeared at the edge of the bed.

Trish sniffed and wiped her eyes with a tissue. "No, those kids upstairs reminded me of my dad, that's all."

"Watching someone die is really rough, no matter what age they are." The nurse handed Trish another tissue. "That was something special, what you did. Your dad would be proud of you."

"I miss him so bad sometimes, it's like I have a hard time breathing." Trish was grateful for the darkness. Talking was easier when you couldn't see the other person very well. "I get my love of horses from him, you know."

"You're fortunate to have had a father like that. He must have been a pretty special man."

"Yep." Trish swallowed her tears, grateful for the compassionate woman holding her hand. "He was." When the silence stretched into comforting peace, the nurse squeezed Trish's hand one last time and left the room.

———

In the morning Trish felt as if everyone were deliberately working in slow motion. It was ten o'clock before the nurse wheeled her patient down to the hospital entrance, and she'd been ready since seven. Keeping a rein on her temper had been as hard as keeping Gatesby from nipping.

"Thanks, Sue. You've been a godsend." Marge

hugged the young nurse before opening the car door.

"Y'all take care now." Sue set the locks on the wheelchair and flipped the footrests upright. "I don't want to see your face here again. I'd much rather come to the track and cheer you on."

Trish waved goodbye, not regretting her farewells in the least. If she never went to a hospital again, it would be too soon.

She closed her eyes and sent prayers for Firefly winging upward. Every time she'd awakened through the night, she'd done the same. Red had called back with reassurances after talking with the vet. As he'd said, leave it to the media to hype the situation.

"We could go to the motel first."

"Right." Trish didn't bother to open her eyes. Seeing Firefly in person would not be put on hold for anything.

Marge stopped the car in the space closest to the veterinarian clinic entrance. "You've got to take it easy, you know."

"Moth-er!" The one word said it all.

They entered the brick building and stopped at the receptionist's desk.

"We're here to see Firefly," Trish answered in response to the woman's greeting.

"Have a seat and I'll get Doctor Grant." The woman's smile was wasted on Trish.

"No, just take me back to see my horse." Trish started toward the door marked PRIVATE.

"Trish." Marge grabbed for her daughter's arm and missed.

The door opened just as Trish raised her hand to push against it. The man in a white thigh-length lab coat could have doubled as a pro-football linebacker.

"You must be Trish Evanston." He held out his hand. "I'm Doctor Grant."

Trish remembered her manners before her mother could deal out a poke-in-the-back reminder. "Glad to meet you."

"Come right this way." He gestured toward an office with chairs arranged in front of a polished teak desk.

"I want to see Firefly—now." Trish met him stare for stare, refusing to be intimidated by his size and soft southern drawl. *Just get out of my way,* she thought. *I've had about all I can take of interfering doctors.*

Dr. Grant shrugged and shifted his attention to Marge as she raised her eyebrows.

"Firefly *is* her horse," Marge said softly.

Trish debated pushing past him, but this wasn't an ordinary vet's office. This place was huge, with corridors running three ways and voices coming over intercoms— just like a regular hospital for humans. She tapped her foot instead. Besides, he looked big and tough enough to subdue a raging stallion, let alone a slightly damaged seventeen-year-old jockey.

"You catch more flies with honey than vinegar," Marge murmured right near Trish's ear. It was one of her mother's pet sayings. But right now Trish wasn't in the mood for flies.

"Right this way." Dr. Grant shrugged one shoulder before he turned and guided them through a labyrinth of white walls and tiled floors. The door he finally opened led into a dimly lit room with high ceilings and a rubberized floor. In the center, suspended in a sling from overhead pulleys, hung a terribly sick sorrel thoroughbred.

"Firefly?" Except for the star on her forehead, Trish

would have doubted the rough-coated animal was really her filly. "Firefly?" At the second call the horse pricked her ears and raised her drooping head an inch or so.

Trish crossed the room to stand by the horse's head. "Oh, my girl, what have they done to you?" She smoothed the filly's forelock and rubbed the slack ears. Firefly leaned her head into Trish's arms and sighed.

Trish wrinkled her nose at the odor of decay that rose like a miasma around her. The smell was only dimmed by the disinfectants used by the hospital. The filly's broken foreleg sported a cast from hoof to shoulder. She'd lost enough weight that even the cast gaped at the top and her ribs stuck out. The gallant spirit that usually beamed from her eyes had gone into hiding.

Trish murmured encouraging words into the filly's ears, all the while agonizing over the deterioration. Could they pull Firefly out of this? Or would it really be better to put her out of her misery?

She felt the doctor by her side before she heard him. "I had planned to prepare you. I know seeing her like this is a shock."

"Umm." Trish continued rubbing the filly's face. "How long since she's eaten or had anything to drink?"

"We keep offering but she refuses. I'd have to check the exact times." He retrieved a metal chart holder from its slot on the wall and returned to her side. He flipped the pages. "Hmm. Two days ago. And she hasn't urinated for eighteen hours, so her kidneys may be shutting down."

"Is that why you said on television last night that you might have to put her down?"

"That wasn't exactly what I said. However, you have to admit that's a strong possibility."

"I don't have to admit anything." Trish squared her shoulders but winced when she took a deep breath. *Why is it people are so ready to give up?* "She'll listen to me and do what I say. Can you get me some warm mash with molasses in it and a bucket of warm water?" She glanced around the room, looking for further inspiration.

"We've already—" The doctor cut off his sentence. "Of course." He and Marge left in deep discussion.

Trish winced when the filly rubbed against her chest. "Easy, girl. That hurts." A stool in the corner caught her attention. But when she moved away, Firefly flung her head in the air and started thrashing around. Trish halted in midstride and spun back to the filly's side. "Easy, easy. You know better than that." Her words and hands worked their magic, but not before the horse's sides heaved in an attempt to draw in sufficient air.

A medical assistant entered the room carrying two stainless steel buckets. "Doctor Grant said to bring you these." She set the buckets down with a clang and tucked a lock of blond hair behind her left ear. "Is there any way I can help you?"

Trish smiled in relief. "Sure. See that stool over there? If I could sit down, I'd be more comfortable. Firefly had a fit when I tried to leave."

"Of course. By the way, my name is Kim. You've been my idol ever since last spring when I watched you win the Derby on Spitfire. What a race!" She carried the stool to Trish while talking.

"Thanks." Trish sat down with a sigh she tried to stifle. "You have a shallow pan or dish anywhere, something I can hold on my lap?"

Kim studied her for a moment. "I'll find something."

While she waited, Trish dipped a handful of water out of the bucket and held it up to the filly's lips. After a second, Firefly lapped the water, slopping some on the floor and more on Trish. At least she was trying. Trish felt the thrill of it tingle clear out to her fingertips. Firefly *would* try for her.

She dipped into the warm mash and held that under the filly's nose. Firefly turned her head away, but when Trish coaxed her again, the horse finally nibbled at the feed.

Dr. Grant returned to stand off to the side. "Drinking is the most important," he said in a hushed tone. He handed her a nearly flat container. Trish poured water into it and drew Firefly's head over so her nose rested in it. Again the filly lapped the water, as if normal drinking were more effort than she could afford. After continued pats and murmurs from Trish, the pan gleamed empty.

"Thank you, God," Marge said softly.

Trish heard her. "Ditto." She dug out a handful of mash and offered it to Firefly. That too disappeared.

"Well, I'll be. Guess those rumors of your gift with horses are true after all." Dr. Grant rocked back on his heels. "Anytime you want to come on staff here, you're welcome. When we tried force-feeding that horse, she went nuts." He turned to his assistant. "Right, Kim?"

"Yeah. I was the one who took a whop on the nose." She rubbed the bridge of her ski-jump nose. "I bled like a stuck hog."

Trish offered the filly another pan of water. This time only half of the liquid disappeared. "She likes it better warm."

Kim left to heat the water.

"I left a message for Patrick. He's probably at the

track." Marge came to stand by Trish's shoulder. "He'll call here with any suggestions he has."

By late afternoon, Trish felt as if she'd been run over by a herd of wild horses. Her ribs ached, her head pounded, and she could have fallen asleep on the stool. But she didn't dare move. Marge brought her a hamburger, fries, and Diet Coke when she complained of a growling stomach.

Every few minutes she offered the filly food and water. Sometimes Firefly took them, but more often she didn't. In between tries, the horse dozed, head down. The sound of her breathing paced Trish's own. When the filly coughed, Trish felt the spasm in her own chest.

When Kim wheeled in an office chair with padded back and arms, Trish smiled gratefully. "Can you take my place, Kim, while I go to the bathroom?" She stood and stretched carefully.

Firefly raised her head. She snorted when Kim sat down on the stool. When Trish backed away the filly nickered. Her hooves rapped a tattoo on the rubber mat, which set the sling to swinging from side to side.

"Stop her! She'll hurt herself!" Kim leaped to the filly's head just in time to take a slam on the chin.

CHAPTER THREE

Kim blinked and shook her head to chase away the stars. She hung on to the horse's halter. "Easy, girl. Come on, you've been doing so well." The filly jerked back and flung her head from side to side.

Trish took Kim's place at the filly's head. "Come on, old girl. I gotta go." Firefly calmed, her head tight against Trish as if locking her into place.

Kim and Trish stared at each other. "What'll we do?" Kim pulled back the stool and sank down on it, rubbing her chin at the same time. "She'll hurt herself again, flailing like that."

"What's happening?" Dr. Grant rushed into the room. At the look of shock on Trish's face, he grinned at her. "No, I'm not omniscient. We have a monitoring system so we can keep track of the animals when we aren't in the room with them. Much like the ones parents use with babies."

"Oh." Trish tried to think if she'd said anything she didn't want overheard.

"So she has a temper tantrum when you try to leave, huh?"

Trish nodded. "Guess I'll have to spend the night with her too."

Marge groaned. "I knew it. You're not going to follow the doctor's orders one bit."

Trish continued stroking the filly. What could they do? At least she'd been able to leave Spitfire in the care of others, though he had tossed any rider besides Trish. Were these two opinionated horses related—or what?

The vet whispered in Kim's ear and, after nodding to the others, left the room. Kim followed him out.

Trish sank back down on the stool, wondering how they were going to handle this. In a few minutes Kim returned with a folding screen, which she set up near the chair. The filly never even flicked a whisker. A bit later another one of the helpers brought in a folding chair with a hole in the seat.

Kim whispered in Trish's ear. "Your rest room awaits—including a window for your friend here so she can see you at all times."

Trish heard a chuckle from behind her. Only her mother laughed like that.

Trish shot her giggling parent a severe look. "You better never tell *anyone* about this or I'll—I'll . . ." She couldn't say any more. Trying to keep from laughing when your ribs ache and you have to go made other actions downright impossible.

Sometime later the helper brought in another chair, one that folded out into a bed.

"That looks familiar," Marge said, "although that certainly wasn't what I'd planned for this night. I rented a perfectly good bed for you at the motel." She stopped Trish's sputter with a raised hand. "I know you can't leave—I don't expect it—but don't gripe when you need to wash your hair again."

Trish shot her mother an exasperated look. She was

glad someone could find some humor in the situation.

———

Kim hung another bottle on the IV hook before leaving for the night. "I'll see you in the morning. John is on night duty this week, so if you need anything, he's the one who'll respond. Red Holleran called and said he'd be here about seven. Wish I could stay—he's about my favorite jockey—but I have class tonight." She looked around at the collection of bedding, the chairs, and the card table where Trish could study and eat. At the moment Trish was encouraging Firefly to drink some more from the shallow basin.

"Thanks for all your help." Trish looked over her shoulder and smiled. "You gotta admit this hasn't been your usual case."

"Well, if you can just get her to pee, we'll all celebrate. She's got a good chance then—if we can clear up the infection and keep her away from pneumonia, that is."

By the time Red and Marge left that night, Trish felt like collapsing on the bed that was now ready for her weary body. Instead she held out the water pan one more time. "Come on, girl, you gotta drink. Patrick says we're doing all we can. Healthy horses need gallons of water a day, you know. And you're running a fever, so you need even more. How will you ever get to go home if you don't drink?"

But Firefly just turned her head, her eyes drooping shut.

Trish crawled between the sheets on the makeshift bed. Things certainly weren't going according to plan— her plan anyway. She watched the filly dozing in the dim light. "Please, God," she whispered, "you're the only one who can help her now. I don't know how many prayers you get to help a horse pee, but that's what we need most right now—that and making her all well again. That infection is really bad. My dad said you care about everything that concerns us, and this sure scares me." The filly snorted and coughed, a dry hacking sound that made Trish's throat hurt just listening. "Thanks for listening and for making me better, too. Amen."

She knew she'd hear every sound the filly made. It looked to be a long night ahead.

About midnight, she gingerly sat up, her muscles warning her she'd had better ideas in her life. Moving slowly and stretching with great care, she scooted the stool back beside Firefly and after filling the basin from the thermos, she held it up for the filly to drink.

"Good girl." Trish set the nearly empty basin on the floor and rubbed the filly's ears. "You did great." Firefly rested her muzzle on Trish's knees and let her eyes close.

"You two all right?" John Adams, with skin as black as his lab coat shone white, crossed from the door on silent feet. He moved with the easy presence of one used to calming sick animals and spoke in the same soothing tone Trish's father had taught her to use.

Firefly didn't even open her eyes, just flicked one ear.

"She drank about a quart that time. That's the most so far."

"Ah'm glad for you, little lady. She wouldn't drink anything for me." He put his stethoscope in his ears and applied the round end to the filly's ribs and chest. "Thank God her lungs are still clear. That's a miracle in itself." He stroked the rough hair under the horse's limp mane. "She's gone through a lot. Last night I wouldn'ta given her half a chance, but now?" He shrugged. "Who knows? You call out if you need anything. The monitors are always on."

Trish crawled back in bed after he left the room. Part of her prayer was being answered. "Thanks, God. Please keep it up."

The sound of splattering water woke her the next time. John burst through the door as Trish catapulted from her bed. "She's peeing! Firefly, you beautiful doll, you. You peed." Trish ignored the complaining from her rib cage and wrapped both arms around the horse's neck.

"Thank God for big blessings," John murmured while he checked the filly again. "Looks like her kidneys are back in production and we're on the right track. Hallelujah." He poured water in the basin and pointed to the stool so Trish could sit and hold it. Firefly drained it, then drank another half. When she raised her head, she snorted drops of water all over Trish.

"Yeah, I know I need a shower, but that wasn't the kind I had in mind." Trish handed the basin back to John and rubbed the star on Firefly's forehead. "Keep up the good work, girl, and we might get home before Christmas yet."

Everyone came by to cheer them on as the good news passed from person to person when they came to work in the morning. Firefly was on the mend. No one even mentioned the idea of her worsening again.

Trish fought back a lump in her throat at the caring the staff exhibited for both her and the filly. If any of her horses ever again needed surgery, she knew where she'd want it to be done.

Three days later Firefly's temperature was near normal, and she was eating and drinking as if to make up for lost time.

"I think you can take some time off now, Trish," Dr. Grant said on his late-afternoon check. "She's much calmer."

"I sure could do with a shower . . ."

"I know—and wash your hair. I have a fifteen-year-old daughter at home. Our water bill doubled when she discovered showers and clean hair."

"Yeah, my dad said he was grateful we had well water when David and I turned teenagers." Trish continued stroking her filly. Firefly especially loved rubs all around her ears.

Kim took over the rubbing duty when Trish eased out the door. The filly snorted once and then leaned into Trish's substitute. Trish breathed a sigh of relief. She'd begun to feel as if she were being held captive—by a sick horse no less. One good thing—she'd gotten all her homework caught up, even the latest assignments her teachers had mailed.

Two days later, after a checkup with the surgeon, she and her mother drove east on the highway to Lexington and BlueMist Farms.

"Now, I hope you don't plan on riding Spitfire while we're there." Marge broke into Trish's half doze.

"Umm—ah . . ." What could Trish say? She'd just been dreaming about cantering Spitfire around the tree-rimmed track at BlueMist.

"You know what the doctor said."

"Umpfm." So much for being a heroine who saved her dying horse. Now she was back to being Trish, daughter of a mother who thought all doctors' orders were just that—orders. Trish liked to consider them more in the line of suggestions—to be followed if convenient.

"I'll take that as a yes."

"Spitfire'll think I don't love him anymore."

"Right."

Trish gazed out at the fields criss-crossed by black board fences. On the crest of the rise, a horse barn with three cupolas stood silhouetted against the blue sky. *What would it be like to own a farm here?* she thought. *Such a difference between my part of the country and this.* She closed her eyes to see Spitfire in one of the paddocks, one owned by her. Then she could ride whenever she wanted to—and see the great black colt everyday.

"Just visiting is the pits."

"Sorry. Maybe you can come back over Christmas break." Marge eased up on the accelerator for the turn into BlueMist. "I know one thing, I need to get home. Bookwork is piling up, and leaving Patrick with all the work just isn't fair."

"I know." Trish dropped her pity cloak as if it were on fire. "But I can't leave until we get Firefly to Blue-Mist."

Now it was Marge's turn to agree. "I'll call for a flight—on the condition that you do what the doctor said."

Trish slapped down the thought that leaped into her mind. Yes, she'd act like a responsible grown-up and mind the doctor—no matter how much it hurt. But oh, to sneak off and ride just for a few minutes. To feel her horse surging beneath her, hear his snorts as he fought the bit, wanting to run full out as badly or worse than she did, the clean smell of fall overlaid with sweaty horse—that was what she wanted.

And what she couldn't have. She loosened her seat belt before the car had come to a full stop in the parking lot by the stallion barn. At the same moment as she opened the car door, her three-toned whistle lifted into the breeze.

A hesitant whinny, as if Spitfire didn't really believe he heard right, answered her. Trish whistled again. This time the colt whistled back, a full-throated stallion's call. He neighed again, the sound lifting and winging its way to Trish, a joyous song of welcome.

Trish took two steps into a trot and thought the better of it. Even whistling hurt her insides—along with the outside.

"Welcome back, lass." Timmy O'Ryan, Spitfire's personal groom and handler, held the door open for her with one hand, tipping his porkpie hat in greeting with the other. "Himself isn't being very patient, but I'm sure that's no surprise to ye."

"Thanks, Timmy, I couldn't wait to see him either." Trish crossed the wide-planked floor in a rush. "Hey, fella, it hasn't been that long since I saw you."

Spitfire leaned against the blue web gate, stretching his neck and muzzle out as far as possible to reach her. His nostrils quivered in a soundless nicker, his ears nearly touching at the tips.

Trish brushed his long, thick forelock to the side before wrapping both arms around his neck. Then she turned and let him drape his head over her shoulder, his favorite pose in all the world. Who knew which of their sighs was greater, or more heartfelt? Trish felt them both clear down to the tips of her tennies.

"Missed me, did you?" Her question right in his ear made his ear twitch. He tipped his head a bit so she could scritch up around his ears more easily.

"Now if that isn't a familiar picture." Marge crossed the room, her heels tapping against the wood. She glanced down the aisle to the other stallions, all with their heads hanging out of their stalls, watching the proceedings. "I'm surprised you haven't charmed the rest of them by now."

"Give her another day," Timmy said under his breath.

Trish looked at him and grinned. She'd made great strides in getting acquainted with the other studs the last time she was at BlueMist.

"I'm going on up to the house now," Marge said. "Why don't you call when you need a ride, but don't be too long. I'm sure dinner will be ready soon."

"Supper, you mean. Remember, we're in the Midwest now." Trish teased her mother, all the while continuing her stroking of the great black colt.

"I'll bring her up. I have to talk to Donald anyway." Timmy returned from the refrigerator with a handful of carrot pieces and gave them to Trish. "We shouldn't be much longer."

"See you later, then." Marge headed back for the door.

"Tell Patrick hi for me if you call him before I get there." Trish kept one carrot piece closed tightly in her fist so Spitfire had to plead for it. Instead of licking her hand, though, he nibbled with his teeth. "Ouch! You be careful."

"Don't tease him, then." Marge left on those words of wisdom.

"Here, lass." Timmy brought a blue canvas director's chair and set it beside her. "I been through smashed ribs enough times to know that you're still hurtin'. You sit here and let that big lug hold his own head up."

With a sigh of relief, Trish did as he suggested. She couldn't have stood much longer, and yet she didn't want her mother to know how badly it hurt or how tired she really was.

"I want you to know, lass, that the Shipsons, me, and some of the others have been praying for you all along. Ye cut ten years off my life, ye did, when you and the filly took that fall. I been there. I know what it's like. I thank my God every day that ye're up and about again." He leaned forward in the chair he'd set down beside Trish's. "Seein' ye here like this . . ."

Trish felt the tears well up and burn at the back of her eyes. *How good everyone is to me! How can I ever thank them enough?* She swallowed and leaned her cheek against Spitfire's forehead. "Thank you." The words seemed so inadequate.

"Well, we better get a move on or ye'll have me blubberin' like a baby." He rose to his feet and put his chair away. "And if I don't get you up there, Sarah'll have my hide for sure."

Trish gave Spitfire a last hug and pushed his nose away so she could get up. "I'll see you in the morning, okay?" Spitfire lipped her cheek, tickling her with his whiskery upper lip. "Oh, gosh, fella, it's so good to see you." She buried her face in his mane one last time before heading for the door.

When she looked back, Spitfire stood with his head up, looking every inch the champion he was. His nicker carried after her out the door.

The fragrance of burning leaves overlaid the clean aroma of fall as the truck wound up the incline to the house set on the hill. Trish caught her breath as she always did when the four white pillars gracing the front of the colonial mansion came into view. Stately trees lined the drive and a monstrous magnolia shaded a round bed of rust and gold chrysanthemums. To the right, wicker furniture invited all who entered to come "set a spell."

If she closed her eyes for even an instant, she could picture women in wide hooped skirts and parasols walking to and fro, laughing and chatting, just like in *Gone with the Wind*. She paused in the portico long enough to look up at the beveled glass and brass hanging light. Surely at one time those flame bulbs had been candles.

Timmy held the heavy walnut door open for her and signaled that she should enter before him. His actions made her feel just the tiniest like a young woman from long ago. She followed the voices she could hear coming from Donald Shipson's office, off to the right.

The sound of her mother's words stopped her as if she'd walked into a glass wall.

"I thought it was all over with, and here is another one." Marge's voice rose a notch. "Why would anyone treat Trish this way? Why?"

Why indeed? Trish felt that old familiar punch in the gut. It barely missed her ribs.

CHAPTER FOUR

The Jerk! He's at me again!

The low rumble of Donald Shipson's voice sounded as if he was trying to calm her mother, but his words were unintelligible.

"So it's only a letter. Next time it might be more than . . ." Marge cut off her cry before it became a shout.

Trish couldn't have moved if ordered by the President himself. Her feet might as well have been nailed to the burnished oak floor. When she raised her gaze from studying the cuticles on her right hand, she caught it on Timmy's compassionate eyes.

He took a step nearer and laid a hand on her shoulder. The warmth of it sank into one of the steel tendons keeping her from flying into a million minute fragments. The Jerk was still around and he'd even gotten the address of BlueMist Farms. Had he sent one of his cheerful little notes to the hospital, too? The thoughts sent shudders rocketing up and down her body.

"Just don't tell Trish, okay?" Her mother's voice had risen again.

Right! The look she got from Timmy clearly asked if she wanted to make their presence known. Trish shook her head. Timmy tiptoed back to the front door and opened it.

41

"They'll be in the office, I'm sure." He raised his voice as if they'd just come in.

Trish picked up the cue like a seasoned stage actress. "Thanks for the ride up. If you see my mom, tell her I'm going to my room to wash for di—supper." She caught the mistake as if it were something critical. She headed for the stairs and turned on the third riser. "See you in the morning, but probably not at the crack of dawn." Amazing how she could project her voice if needed. All the while her jaw felt as if it were clamped in a vise.

Timmy nodded and sent her a smile and a thumbs-up before walking to the half-closed office door and tapping with two fingers.

Trish trudged on up the wide walnut stairs, turning at the landing before she took hold of the railing with her left hand. She used it to help pull herself the remainder of the way up. Each step took an effort nearly beyond her strength. And this morning she had felt as if she could climb Mt. Hood. Right.

How would she bring up the questions about this person who insisted on intruding in her life? Who was he? Could it be a she? That thought hadn't entered her mind before. No girl would do something like this—would she?

Trish stumbled across the rose-patterned rug to the white canopied bed. Maybe if she would just lie down a couple of minutes she would feel like getting ready for dinner—supper—whatever. Knowing Sarah, the food would be terrific. But right now, the thought of food of any kind made her throat tighten. How could she possibly join the Shipsons and her mother and not let them know she knew?

She needn't have worried. By the time she opened

her eyes, pitch black night had fallen, and she felt her mother carefully removing her shoes.

"What time is it?" Trish finally recovered her alertness enough to ask.

"A bit after nine. I came up to get you for supper and you were sleeping so soundly, I just covered you and left. But I thought you'd sleep better without all your clothes on."

"Thanks." Trish let her eyelids drift shut again, but immediately the conversation she'd overheard from the office rang in her ears. "Mom, I want you to tell me the truth about what's going on." Trish sat up, swung her legs over the edge of the bed, and snapped on the lamp next to the bed. She began unbuttoning her shirt so she could keep her hands busy.

Marge stood upright. "Of course."

"You—we've heard from The Jerk again, haven't we?"

Her mother sank to the edge of the bed and helped Trish remove her clothes. "Yes, we have."

"Why didn't you tell me?"

"Oh, Tee, we felt it was so important you get better without worrying that we decided to . . . to . . ."

"Lie to me?"

"Not exactly. We just didn't tell you."

"How many?"

"Two cards sent to the hospital and now this one here. Amy and Officer Parks are still working on the case on the Portland end. We send them anything we get." She retrieved Trish's PJ's from the duffel bag and held the top so Trish could put her arms in without straining her sides. "How did you guess?"

"No guess. Timmy and I heard you when we came up to the house. I thought I'd try to let you keep the secret, but it was too hard. Besides, Dad always said the truth is easier to deal with than a lie." She leveled an accusing stare in her mother's direction. "I *am* an adult now, you know."

The smile that barely lifted the corners of Marge's mouth matched her wistful tone. "I keep trying to re-member that, but to me, you're still my baby, my only daughter, and I want to protect you from all the evil things in this world. That's a mother's job, you know, to take care of her kids." She gave Trish a hug and followed it by a kiss on the cheek. "I love you, Tricia Marie Ev-anston, and too often you scare the livin' out of me."

What could Trish say? She leaned her head against her mother's shoulder. The light from the rose-painted Tiffany lamp glowed softly, feeling warm and loving like her mother's touch. Before she fell all the way back asleep, Trish pushed herself upright and crawled under-neath the covers, shoving the white lace-edged pillows off to the side. "Night, Mom."

Marge rose and dropped a kiss on her daughter's forehead. "Good-night, Tee. Just remember, God loves you and so do I." For a change, the words her father al-ways said didn't bring a lump to Trish's throat. She drifted off thinking, *Thank you, God*, but too far gone to voice the words.

———

In the morning after visiting Spitfire, Trish joined the Shipsons and her mother at the dining table. Sarah, the longtime cook for BlueMist, brought in a platter of sliced ham with fluffy scrambled eggs. A basket of bis-cuits already graced the center of the white-linen-covered table. An icy glass of fresh-squeezed orange juice held the place of honor above Trish's plate.

"Any time you want to move to the West Coast, you just let us know." Trish grinned up at the woman serving them.

"Chile, y'all couldn't bribe me away from here. This been mah home far too long. But y'all know, you're welcome anytime." She plopped two slices of ham and a mound of scrambled eggs on Trish's plate. "Now eat up and get yo strength back. Y'all lookin' mighty puny."

Trish stared at all the food on her plate. "You want me to get so fat I can't ride anymore?" Her voice rose to a squeak. But all the time she was complaining and teasing, her hands were busy draping her snowy napkin across her lap and cutting up the ham. The biscuits appeared at her side, and she flipped two of them over to join the ham and eggs.

"And I have coffee cake comin' outa the oven for when you finish with this." Sarah handed the platter to Bernice Shipson and marched back out of the room.

"You better eat up. She's been known to pout for days when someone refuses her food." The twinkle in Donald Shipson's blue eyes belied his words. "And you wouldn't want to wish that on any of us."

"I'll try my best, sir." Trish saluted and dug in.

Stuffed to the tips of her ears, Trish turned away the second piece of cinnamon-and-sugar-topped coffee cake Sarah encouraged her to take. "I can't. You cut them like slabs for a football team."

"Half then." Sarah whacked the four-by-four square in two and slid one onto Trish's plate.

Trish groaned and shook her head at the laughter from around the table. "How come she doesn't pick on any of you?"

"You should have seen the way she mollycoddled Donald when he broke his leg one time." Bernice leaned forward, her silver-blond hair swinging forward on her cheek. "Nearly drove him nuts."

Marge glanced at her watch. "I better get myself on the road if I'm going to make that flight. Trish, you sure you won't come with me?"

Trish's "Mo—ther" conveyed all the nuances possible and then some.

"Before you go"—Donald laid his folded napkin back on the table—"I talked with Doctor Grant, and he thinks we can transport Firefly in another three or four days, that is if Trish is up to it."

"Of course." Trish looked from him to her mother.

"You could get bumped around," Marge cautioned.

"Yeah, but probably not. She'll do just fine. You'll see." Trish got to her feet, being very careful not to flinch at the movement. She came around the table and gave her mother a hug. "Pass one of these on to Patrick for me, okay? And Miss Tee might like extra attention by now too." Trish referred to her nearly two-year-old filly who'd been born on her birthday last September. All thoroughbreds' birthdays are officially counted as January first, so Miss Tee would be considered two in January.

———

The days passed quickly with Trish spending much of her time down in the stallion barn with Spitfire. Red came out to visit one evening, but he couldn't stay long since he had to be on the track again at five A.M.

The next morning, Donald Shipson drove Trish and Timmy into Louisville to bring Firefly back. A taller than normal horse van was already backed in place by the veterinary hospital. Dr. Grant met them at the filly's room.

"As you can see, we've designed a walking cast that she can hobble, or rather, limp along with." He pointed to the contraption that went from under the filly's hoof to above her shoulder. "While we feel she would do well in the sling at least part time once you're at BlueMist, this makes her more portable. Since the infection is cleared up and the incision's healing well, the plates in her leg are really what protect her. The cast is just to keep her from banging it around."

Trish walked up to the nickering filly and rubbed her face and ears. "You old sweety, you. What a difference a couple of days make. You look almost like your old self, at least you would without that rig on your leg." Firefly scrubbed her forehead against Trish's shoulder. "Easy. You'll have us both on the ground if we're not careful." She dug in her pocket for a chunk of carrot. Firefly never hesitated for a second, just lipped it and crunched.

"Trish, I take it you are going to ride in the van with your horse?" the doctor asked.

Trish nodded.

"I've arranged for Kim to go along with you, sedative prepared, just in case Firefly becomes agitated again."

"She won't."

"Well, I live by my mother's oft-said 'better safe than sorry,' so I'm trying to cover all the bases." He turned to Donald, who'd been standing to the side. "I've already talked with your own Doctor Tyler this morning, and he'll be at the farm when you arrive. Your driver can call him from the truck."

"I have a cellular phone, so that's no problem," Donald answered. "And he'd already discussed this with me."

"Fine. Let's begin. Getting her in and out of the trailer will be the real trick."

Trish unbuckled the halter and handed it to Kim. With Timmy on one side and Trish on the other, they slipped a leather headstall in place and adjusted the two chain leads over Firefly's nose and under her chin so both of them would have a strap.

"I'm just back-up," Timmy sang to the filly, much like Trish did. The two of them made a fine duet.

"Okay, girl. Let's show them how smart you are." Trish took one step backward and then another. With one hand scratching the horse's cheek, she tugged on the lead with the other.

Firefly lurched forward, one ungainly step at a time. Dr. Grant, Kim, Donald, and another attendant acted like spotters for a gymnast, ready to lend their strength to keep the filly on her feet.

By the time they reached the wide-open double doors, Trish could feel the sweat trickling down her back. Dark wet spots were popping out on the filly's neck, evidence of the strain she was under.

"Come on, girl, you're doing fine." Trish let the hobbling horse pause in the open doorway and sniff the breeze. The bright sun made them all blink. "Feels like I've run five miles—with a forty-pound pack."

"You've never really done that—have you?" Donald ran a comforting hand over the filly's rump.

"No, but . . ."

"Well, I have," Dr. Grant added. "In the army—and it nearly killed me. Wouldn't wish that on anyone." He walked around the filly, checking the cast and listening to her lungs and heart. "You're a game one, old girl." He patted the sorrel shoulder. "Never would have believed we'd be shipping you out on your own steam."

Trish swapped a look with Timmy that said what they thought of the good doctor's attitude. Trish bit her lower lip to keep from commenting. *He gave up on you, old girl. But you and me, we didn't.* She stroked the filly's sweaty neck. *And God didn't. Thank you, Father.*

"We better keep her moving or she'll stiffen up. I want to get a blanket on her soon's possible." Timmy motioned for Trish to step out again.

They worked their way the few feet to the ramp without any problems, but when Firefly put her front feet on the ramp, she shivered.

"Easy, girl, come on, you can do it." Trish kept her voice to the soothing singsong. "That ol' ramp's nearly flat. You'll make it fine."

Another step. Firefly threw her head in the air, in spite of the chain over her nose.

At the upward jerk, Trish gasped at the pain in her side. She let the lead travel through her fingers and worked it back in place again. She swallowed and took a deep breath. Another mistake.

"You all right, lass?" Timmy kept his voice soothing and his hands busy stroking up around Firefly's ears.

"I will be."

Firefly dropped her head and sniffed the ramp. She sucked in a deep breath of air and, on the exhale, nuzzled Trish's arm.

"You ready for more?" Trish raised her gaze to the sky above, catching the flight of a flock of birds against the deep blue. "Sure wish we had some wings here about now."

Timmy grinned at her and nodded. "That would be good." He waited a moment. "You ready?"

Trish nodded. "Okay, girl, all the way." She stepped farther up the ramp and tugged gently on the lead.

Firefly planted her feet and leaned back on her haunches.

"Come on, Firefly, you know better than this." Trish tugged again. The filly's ears were laid back.

Trish released the tension on her lead.

Firefly leaped forward. She slammed into Trish in the rush.

No! Trish kept the scream in her head as she spun off the ramp.

CHAPTER FIVE

Trish grabbed for the rail, the door, anything. Her hands raked across metal.

She kept falling.

"Oof!" Even with a cushion of strong arms and a broad chest, Trish felt the jolt clear through her. She opened her eyes to see Dr. Grant grinning at her as he set her back on the ground. "Th-thanks. That was close."

"Glad I could be of service." The doctor's grin wobbled, looking about like Trish's legs felt. "Young lady, no wonder your mother is getting gray hair. If you'd have crushed those ribs again, she'd have strung me up."

"Hardly." Trish put a hand to her side and leaned forward to breathe more easily. At the same time she rubbed her stomach to get it back down where it belonged. If she looked as pale as she felt, she knew she was in trouble. "She's used to me. Besides, it wasn't my fault. Firefly just got tired of hobbling." Trish stepped up on the ramp and entered the van to find her filly rubbing against Timmy with her bony forehead.

"You okay, lass?" Timmy ducked under the filly's neck to check Trish out.

"I will be. Let's get this show on the road." *So I can lie down for a while* was the thought deliberately kept unspoken.

"Why don't you go sit in that chair and let us take care of your horse?" Kim joined Trish beside the filly.

"I will as soon as we get her settled." She turned to Dr. Grant. "Thanks for all you've done for her—and for being such a good catcher."

"Glad we could help." Dr. Grant gave Donald an assist with the quilted traveling sheet, smoothing a hand down Firefly's back after securing the last of the buckles. "Hope to see you at Churchill Downs again next year."

As soon as they were underway, Trish let herself sink into the canvas chair against the far wall. She closed her eyes, gently rubbing her side at the same time. That seemed to ease the pain. What she wouldn't give for some aspirin right then.

The trip to BlueMist passed without any further incident. At one point Timmy touched Trish's shoulder and pointed to a pile of horse blankets. She roused herself enough from the drowse she'd been hovering in and curled up on the pads. *How come pain can make you so sleepy?* The thought never had time for an answer because she sank beyond drowse like a stone falling into a pool.

———

Trish spent the next day alternating between Firefly's and Spitfire's stalls. During a thunderstorm in the afternoon she stayed with Spitfire. While he'd gotten somewhat used to the crashing storm, loud noises still spooked him.

"Easy, fella, it's just thunder," Trish crooned to him after a particularly close strike. Her eardrums still echoed from the boom. *If you were home, you wouldn't have to put up with such stuff.* The thought made her wince.

Her mother had called last night wondering when Trish was flying in. They'd agreed on Saturday, only the day after next.

If only Spitfire could be brought back to Vancouver. Trish leaned her forehead against his neck. "Guess that's the price of fame," she whispered. "Only how come it has to hurt so much?"

Spitfire turned and nuzzled her shoulder. When that didn't get her attention, he lipped the braid hanging down her back.

"Ouch." She pushed his nose away. "You don't have to get so rough." He threw his head up and rolled his eyes, the whites gleaming bright in the gloom. "Sure, I know, you're scared to death." Another flash of lightning glinted through the windows. "Hang on, here we go again." She turned so he could rest his head over her shoulder and placed a hand over the ridge of his nose.

Trish counted. But this time, the thunder took five seconds to boom after the lightning flash. The storm was quickly moving away from them. Spitfire only flinched, his hide rippling beneath her hand.

Once the rain let up, she crossed the gravel parking lot to the quarantine barn, where Firefly occupied a double stall so she could have plenty of room to move around. José, one of the grooms, stayed with her to make sure she didn't try to lie down.

"How ya doin'?" Trish asked the aging former jockey.

"Not bad. She's a good horse, that one. Shame she won't run again."

"At least she's alive." Trish stroked the filly's neck. "Much as I'd love to see her on the track, she'll make a good broodmare." She tickled the filly's whiskery upper lip. "Won't you, girl?" Firefly snuffled Trish's pockets looking for her treat. When she found the right one, she nosed harder. "Okay, okay, be patient will you?" Trish drew the carrot out of her jacket pocket and let the horse munch away. The crunch of carrot coupled with the water dripping through the downspouts sang a kind of tune. One of peace and contentment.

Trish took her American government textbook out of her book bag and sank down in the corner of the stall to study. "You can take a break now if you'd like. I'll be here for an hour at least." She listened while José left the building. When his footsteps faded, she leaned her head back against the wall. Firefly snuffed Trish's hair and then rested her nose against Trish's shoulder, the horse's eyes drifting closed.

Trish let her book dangle between her bent knees. Vancouver, Portland Meadows, Prairie High School— they all seemed light years away. What would it be like to stay in Kentucky? She'd be closer to major tracks, that's for sure. Probably even head down to Florida when Donald shipped his string down there. She could be at BlueMist when Spitfire serviced the mares that other breeders would bring in. Spend time in the foaling barns. Go to school.

She shook her head. No, her senior year took priority. She shut off the daydreams and reopened her book. Graduating with her friends *was* important. After all, she'd never be seventeen again. She had plenty of years to race.

Now she sounded like her mother. Trish's snort made Firefly jerk up her head. "Easy, girl. You can go back to sleep. I'll be careful."

She called Rhonda that evening to let her in on the latest plans.

"You mean you're *finally* coming home?" Trish could just picture Rhonda, flat on her bed with one knee cocked over the other.

"You mean you've missed me? What about that tall, handsome basketball player who takes all your spare time?"

"Jason *is* rather nice."

"Nice?" Trish choked on the word. "I'll tell him what you said."

"You know, he plays basketball every day after school, and he's even found a weekend league. So, it's like I never get to see him."

"Right!"

"Besides that, I've had shows nearly every weekend. Which reminds me—you haven't seen me jump once this fall."

Guilt dealt Trish a blow to the midsection. "Sorry."

"Not your fault, but I qualified for the Pan Pacific, so you better clear those days. That's my entry into the big time."

The two chatted a few more minutes before Trish hung up. Yeah, it was time to go home. She'd missed out on a lot.

Friday night Red arrived right on time to take her out to supper. "How does Barney's Ribs sound?" he asked on their way down the steps.

"Sounds good to me. We don't get real southern barbequed ribs in Vancouver."

"That's what I thought. Then maybe a movie—or just a drive?"

"Up to you." She wanted to add, *I just like being with you,* but the words stuck in her throat. She'd have thought with her being in Kentucky she would have seen more of him, but a popular jockey didn't have a lot of extra time. Now, if she'd been at the track . . .

Before their dinner was served, Red had signed three autographs, and when the fans realized Trish was with him, they kept both jockeys busy.

Trish smiled at a young girl who had braces glinting on her teeth and who swore she'd be a jockey someday just like Trish. "Spend all the time you can learning to ride and handle horses," Trish told her. "Any kind of horse. And keep up your schoolwork so you get good grades." Trish could hardly believe she'd said that. Must be her mother's coaching coming out.

By the time they left the restaurant, it was too late to do more than head back to BlueMist. The golden harvest moon sailed above the tops of the trees, gilding branches and rooftops and casting deep shadows.

"Wish you could stay here." Red took her hand in his.

"I've thought about it. The Shipsons invited me, too." The warm fuzzies inched up her arm and around her heart. Was this what love felt like?

"And?"

"And I have to go home. Mom needs me, and so does Runnin' On Farm. Besides, I want to graduate with my class." She laid her head on his shoulder.

"But you'll come back?"

"Of course. But I've got a lot of races to run out there, you know." She smiled up at him. "You could come west and ride."

"It would have to be California."

"I know. Portland doesn't pay very well. But the Meadows has been good to me."

Red snorted.

Trish knew he was thinking about the mess at the

track when she'd been shot at. "But that's all over now."

"Sure." He snorted again.

The thought of The Jerk snapped her head up from its resting place. "We're going to get him." She put all the confidence she could into her reply.

"It better be soon." Red kissed her good-night and hugged her close. "I gotta admit I worry about you. Please be careful, will you?"

Trish nodded against his shoulder. Why did saying goodbye always make her eyes water?

He dropped another kiss on her nose before opening the door to the mansion for her. "See ya."

She watched him jump down the steps and jog to his pickup. When the taillights disappeared down the drive, she entered the house and shut the door behind her. Major sniffing all the way up the stairs kept the tears at bay.

———

Trish stood in Spitfire's stall the next morning, fighting back the tears, glad Timmy had thought to leave them alone. Saying goodbye to him was never easy. "I know I'll see you again in a few months, so you just behave yourself, you hear?"

Spitfire nodded. He nosed her pocket for the carrot he smelled and blew carrot perfume in her face while he munched. It was when she left the stall that he kicked up a fuss. He snorted and stamped his front feet, then let out a piercing shriek.

Two other stallions answered him from inside the barn and another from his paddock outside.

"Knock it off, you goof." Trish returned to the web gate and shook her finger in front of his face. "You know better than that." Spitfire tried to rub his forehead against her chest, but Trish pushed him away.

"He'll settle down soon as you're out the door." Timmy unhooked the web and entered Spitfire's stall. "You take care of yourself now, lass."

"You suppose he knows I'm leaving for Vancouver?"

"I believe he understands a lot more than we give him credit for." Timmy smoothed the stallion's mane. "Have a good trip."

Saying goodbye to BlueMist was getting harder each time. Trish kept reminding herself she was lucky to have two—no three when you include California—places to call home.

"You'll come again—soon?" Bernice reached over the back of the seat of the Cadillac and patted Trish's knee. "Since you're now our daughter too, we'll just have to bribe Marge to let us have you more often."

"You could attend college here in Kentucky, you know." Donald caught her eye from his rearview mirror.

Trish grimaced at the thought. "I'm not sure about college. I know my mom plans for me to go next fall, but I'd rather ride. I can go back to college any time."

"Or part time. Some of the jockeys do that." Bernice turned in her seat so she could see Trish.

"It's hard to know what to do."

"Rest assured, God will let you know, if you ask." She rested one arm on the back of the burgundy leather seat. "And, my dear, you certainly have all kinds of options."

Trish nodded. "I know." She knew this discussion would be coming up at home and her mother would *not* be as understanding. To Marge, education was *the* most important thing, right up there next to faith. No matter how much her mother was now involved in the horses and managing Runnin' On Farm, changing her views on college would be like stopping the mighty Columbia River with one hand.

———

In fact, the college discussion came up the next evening. After attending church in the morning, Trish spent the afternoon at the track. Now she was sitting in her father's recliner in front of a blazing fire in the fieldstone fireplace that covered most of one wall in the living room. Brad Williams lay stretched out on the floor, studying for one of his college classes. Rhonda Seaboldt, queen of the couch, was pushing her flyaway red hair back so she could wrap a band around it. Her government book lay open in her cross-legged lap.

Marge brought in cups of hot chocolate and a plate of chocolate chip cookies. "Now this is as pretty a picture as I've seen anywhere." She offered the tray to each of the kids.

"Been a long time, hasn't it?" Brad pushed himself upright and took a cup along with a handful of cookies. "Thanks, Mrs. E. You sure know the way to a man's heart."

"Sure. Give you cookies and you'll do anything." Trish snapped her book shut and set it on the end table. This was one of those times when she felt sure if she turned her head quick enough, she'd see her father standing right behind her chair—or rather *his* chair. She could almost feel his hand on her shoulder.

"You talked to David lately?" Brad asked around a mouthful of cookie.

Trish could tell that, as usual, they were all on the same wavelength. The four teens—Trish, David, Brad, and Rhonda—had been inseparable for all their growing-up years. That's why Marge called them her "Four Musketeers."

"He'll be home for Thanksgiving. Says he loves college in Tucson." Marge took her place in her rocker.

"I'm thinking of going there next year." Brad dropped his bombshell into the peace and watched it explode.

"You are!" Trish and Rhonda could have been one person.

"The more I think about it, the more I'd like to become a vet too. David and I could build a practice together." He popped another cookie in his mouth.

Trish and Rhonda swapped startled looks. "But you never . . ." "I thought you . . ." Their comments overlapped. Trish set her mug down and leaned forward. "All right, buddy. When did this all come about?"

"Just lately. I really like helping Patrick with the horses, like I always have, and yet I can't see myself as a trainer."

"So you decided on veterinary."

"With a specialty in horses." He wrapped both arms around his bent knees. "I'm sending off my application tomorrow."

"Speaking of applications . . ." Marge gave Trish one of those this-is-your-mother-reminding-you looks that Trish hated.

"I've filled out three," Rhonda said. "Cal-Poly in San Luis Obispo, Washington State University, and Cal State, Davis." Rhonda chose another cookie from the plate on the coffee table in front of her. "All have good jumping programs. I'll take my horse right with me."

All three of them looked at Trish.

"I don't think I'm going to go to college." Trish raised her chin slightly in her don't-mess-with-me look. But her eyes pleaded, "Please understand."

CHAPTER SIX

The log in the fire snapped like a rifle shot.

"I don't think so." Marge planted her elbows on the arms of the chair. She sucked in a deep breath.

Trish could tell her mother was fighting to keep her cool. Glancing over at Rhonda was a mistake. Her best friend's head shook back and forth and her eyebrows had disappeared into her hairline. Brad seemed to be counting the threads in the weave of his jeans.

"Anyone for more hot chocolate?" Trish had to clear her throat at the end of the sentence. Marge shot her a glance fit to fry eggs. Brad and Rhonda shook their heads.

"We better be headin' out." Brad set his cup on the raised rock hearth in front of the fire, then thought better of it and stood to cross the room, placing his mug carefully on the tray.

"Yeah, yeah, we better." Rhonda copied his moves.

Chickens! Getting while the getting's good. See if I ever bail you out of a family hassle again. But Trish didn't say it, she just nodded. She got to her feet and followed them to the door.

"Thanks for the treats," Rhonda called back.

Marge kind of grunted.

"In the morning?" Brad paused.

"Sure," Marge answered. The one word carried the edge of a newly sharpened knife.

"Thanks for nothing, guys." Trish muttered to her friends' retreating backs.

"See you in the morning, like usual?" Rhonda's question floated back, threading its way through the mist. Rainbows circled the mercury yard light that glinted off the droplets frosting Brad's baby blue Mustang.

Trish took in a deep breath of the cold, wet air, wishing she could go anywhere but back to where her mother could be heard clanking cups. She shut the door and returned to the living room. What was that phrase she'd heard, something about a good offense being the only defense? That wasn't quite right but who cared? Right now she had to deal with a very unhappy mother.

"I know you're disappointed." Trish leaned against the cedar-paneled wall.

With the cups clanked into submission and into the kitchen, Marge was now attacking the sofa cushions.

"But I know this is the right thing for me to do. And if you tried to see it from my point of view, you'd agree." Could looks really send daggers?

Marge strode over to the fire and poked until sparks flew up the chimney in fear.

"Mom, stop all this and talk to me."

She threw in a log, then another.

Trish sat down on the arm of the sofa. Marge now leaned against the mantel, her head resting on her arm. *Dad, where are you? I need you so. Right now.* Trish chewed on her bottom lip. It would be so much easier to just agree with her mother right now. Say, "Sure I'll go to college." But the thought made her heart stop.

Can't you see that I'm first and foremost a jockey? That's my gift, my calling. And after that I may want to be a trainer, like Dad. Or maybe I'll ride until I'm fifty. She stared at the rigid line of her mother's back. *Or maybe I'll just . . . just . . .*

Just what? Even Nagger didn't seem his usual naggy self. *You have to go with what's right for you, kid.*

Trish blinked her eyes. Had she heard right? What would her father do in a situation like this? She rubbed her sore ribs with one hand and her chin with the other, trying to remember.

Dad had always walked over, put his arms around his wife, and said, "No matter how we decide on this, just remember that I love you." Trish fought down the boulder that instantly clogged her throat. She ordered one foot to lead the way and the other to follow. One step at a time, as if she were just learning to walk, she crossed the room.

She put a hand on her mother's shoulder. "Mom, no matter how much we go round on this, just remember that I love you." The words started hard and got easier as they went. "I hate fighting and either one of us being angry."

The shoulder under her hand shuddered. Marge turned, tears caught on the tips of her eyelashes, and she wrapped Trish in a mighty hug.

"Would you consider sending out applications in case you change your mind?" Marge finally asked after they both snagged tissues from the box and blew their noses.

"It would be a waste of their time—and mine. Guess I made the final decision on the plane. I can always go to college later, but my career as a jockey is really building. I should be riding full time now, but I won't because I promised you I'd give my senior year priority. And that's what I want to do too." Trish sank down on the hearth. She watched her mother's emotions play hide-and-seek with the firelight flickering across her face.

"I can't say I'm happy about this."

"I don't expect you to."

"But I do honor your decision about what to do with your life. Your father and I always said we wouldn't force our career decisions on you kids. You do what you feel called for. Our job is to see that you have the most information possible to make a wise decision."

Trish breathed a sigh of relief.

Marge went on. "But you'll have to give me some time. I always dreamed of both you kids graduating from college and exploring new fields. Guess I thought that would make your life more secure. I need time to let go of that dream and tune in to yours. You know that racing is not the safest of sports."

"Mom, you're the best. I know you're angry . . ."

"I'd prefer to say upset . . ." A grin tugged at the corner of Marge's mouth. "And please remind Brad and Rhonda of that fact."

"Oh, I will." Trish glanced over at the picture-perfect-plumped sofa cushions. "And I'm glad you took out your 'upset' on those instead of me."

Marge laid an arm across Trish's shoulders. "Me too." She snapped off the lamp as they passed it. "But I won't promise not to try to change your mind once in a while."

Trish had no trouble coming up with three things to be thankful for that night. In fact, her list stretched beyond ten before she dropped off.

———

Since morning stiffness made dressing take longer, Trish bailed out of bed before her alarm went off. She checked the blazing pink scar three ribs down from her left armpit. Every day both it and raising her arm improved. If she really *had* to, she could probably ride all right next week. Maybe next Saturday she'd head for the track with Patrick and ride for morning works.

She brushed her teeth and opted for leaving her hair down. Raising her arms to braid it still hurt too bad.

Wearing the denim skirt, silk blouse, and boots she and Rhonda had bought in California always raised her self-confidence a notch, and getting back in her own red convertible added another. It seemed like years since she'd driven it, what with the time it spent in the shop for a new paint job. Thinking of the keyed scratches on her car brought back the thought of The Jerk. She shuddered. Where was he? Who was he? Why was he doing this?

When she got to Rhonda's she wrote in her notebook, "Call Amy." It was time they nailed this creature, whoever he was.

Rhonda talked nonstop all the way to school, which was nothing new, bringing Trish up-to-date on everything that had happened. Doug Ramstead, the star quarterback, had pulled a hamstring and missed the last game, but they won anyway.

"He's been asking about you." Rhonda raised her eyebrows suggestively.

"He sent me a couple of cards while I was in the hospital." Trish had her blinker on to turn into the Prairie High parking lot.

"I told you once and I'll tell you again, if you'd give that guy half a chance, he could really like you."

"Yes, Rhonda." Trish completed the turn. "But I like Red, remember?"

"But he's so far away." Rhonda threw up her hands. "We could double-date if you'd . . ."

"We'll see, okay?" Trish parked in what had become her usual place. "Right now I gotta set up a schedule for making up the midterms I missed. I promised my mom I'd keep my grades up, but I hadn't planned on being gone a whole month."

Trish waved and greeted all her friends as she made her way to the office to talk with Mrs. Olson.

"You sure do lead an exciting life," the smiling counselor said. "I've talked with all your teachers and we've made up a schedule: one test a day after school, starting tomorrow." She handed Trish a paper with the list. "You think you're ready for that?"

"Much as I'll ever be. Lying flat on your back gives you plenty of time to study."

"What a scare you gave us all. You aren't planning on racing yet?" Mrs. Olson reached for a pink slip and filled it out, since the warning bell had already rung.

"Probably next week but never during school." Trish got to her feet. "Thanks." She picked up the pink slip and headed for class. Back to normal. Now Kentucky seemed a world or two away.

When Trish and Rhonda entered the cafeteria for lunch, the guys at their table stood up and cheered. Trish felt the blush starting under her collar and blazing across her cheeks. A wolf whistle came from across the room. Trish could feel every eye in the place gazing at her as if she stood under a spotlight.

"I'm gonna murder those guys," she said through gritted teeth, trying to smile at the same time.

"I told you. Doug likes you." Rhonda nudged Trish from behind to get her moving forward in line.

By the end of lunch it was as if she'd never been away. Jason sat on the other side of Rhonda, laughing and teasing like he'd gone to Prairie all his life, not just the last few months as an exchange student. Doug, the dream of nearly every girl in school, sat on Trish's right, teasing her into laughing so hard she flinched.

"Ribs, huh?" He leaned closer and said softly, "I broke mine once, hurts like crazy."

"It's even worse when I laugh or cough, so cool it." Trish nibbled on a carrot stick. "When I'm gone, I forget how crazy you guys are."

He turned to look her in the eye. "Well, how about not being gone so much?" His deep blue eyes crinkled at the edges. "I'm glad you're back."

A shiver ran up Trish's spine. Maybe Rhonda was right after all. "Thanks. I'm glad to be here, and all in one piece."

Doug picked up her books and walked her back to her locker. He leaned one arm against the tan metal door next to hers. "You think while you're laid up, you might find time to see a movie or something with another laid-up jock?" His gaze met hers, then skipped away. Two books fell off the stack in the bottom of the locker and hit the floor. Doug dropped to his knees and picked them up, holding her gaze as he handed them back.

"Please."

"But I . . ."

"Just as friends." He stuck his fingertips in the front pockets of his jeans. The warning bell rang.

"Sure, why not?" Trish grabbed her notebook and

slammed the locker door closed. "I'm free Saturday night. What's playing?"

"Got me." He laid a well-muscled arm across her shoulders.

"No horror or gross stuff."

"Okay."

"And I have to be at the track at five-thirty. That's before sunrise, you know, so I can't stay out late."

Rhonda came up beside her and poked her arm. Trish knew it meant "I told you so." Trish poked her back.

———————

Officer Amy Jones drove into the Runnin' On Farm driveway right behind Trish. She leaped from her sporty green car and threw her arms around Trish. "Hi, kid. I know, I'm hugging carefully." Her actions followed her words. "It's so good to have you home. I wanted to stay longer, but the powers that be thought you'd be safe enough in the ICU."

Trish just hugged her favorite police person back. She didn't try to break into the rushing river of words. She'd never heard Amy run on like this in all the time they'd spent together.

"Trish, you scared the life out of me." Amy gripped Trish's shoulders with both hands. "And there was nothing I could do for you. That's when I knew I had to let God in. Only He could take care of you, and I had to be able to ask."

Trish clasped Amy's hand and squeezed. "Thanks for the cards and flowers—and all the prayers too." She opened the door and motioned for Amy to go in first. "As you can see, they worked."

After greeting Marge and accepting her offer of freshly baked snickerdoodle cookies, Trish and Amy settled in the living room. Amy checked her watch. "Since I'm on a stakeout tonight, we better get busy."

"Not just a friendly call, huh?" Trish nibbled her cookie.

"Nope, I wish. But we need to nail this guy before he does any real damage." She handed Trish a list of names. "These are all the people we've investigated while you were gone."

Trish glanced down the list. "Doug Ramstead? Brad? You've got to be kidding!"

"Nope. In my business no one is exempt." Amy looked down at her list. "See name number sixteen? He's the jockey who whipped your horses during a couple of races last year."

"I know. Emanuel Ortega." Trish looked up from the list. "He went and raced at Yakima last summer. We're not friends, but he's never done anything like that again."

"At least, not that you know of."

"Right."

Trish felt a squiggle of doubt worm its way into her mind. Was everyone she knew a suspect? How could she live with that? "I bet it has something to do with Kendall Highstreet, the developer. Forget my friends and ask him."

"We have, let me assure you." Amy shook her head. "He's clean."

"What about his friends and family?" Trish set her Diet Coke down with a clink. "The people who work for him?"

Amy gave her what could only be called a police officer's patient-but-don't-be-dumb look.

"I'm sorry." Trish leaned back in the recliner. "You've already done that, and I should trust you to do your job."

"You got it." Amy leaned forward, her elbows on her knees. "Trish, please, keep your eyes and ears open and let me know if you see anything unusual. Immediately if not before."

Trish sighed. "I'd hoped it was all over."

"So did I. So did I."

After Amy left, Trish wandered down to the barns to visit with her four-legged friends. Caesar, the farm collie, danced by her side, yipping then running ahead and yipping again. His feathered tail beat a tattoo against her legs when he returned to her side. Trish bent over to get her quick tip-of-the-nose lick.

"Easy, fella. I did wash my face this morning." She buried her fingers in his snowy ruff and swung his head back and forth, the loose skin pushing wrinkles up to his ears and over his pointed head. The sable collie planted his front feet on her shoulders and tried for her nose again. Trish had always said he had the fastest tongue in the West, and in her absence he'd not lost his touch. After what could never be enough roughing, he dashed off and yipped again, running circles around her at lightning speed.

Trish planted her hands on her hips and laughed aloud at his antics. They had come so close to losing him. Had that poisoning been the stalker too? Or was it just an unfortunate accident? "Sure wish you could talk, fella."

Her three-tone whistle floated off on the evening breeze when she rounded the long, low barns and headed down the lane to the paddocks. White board fences lined both sides of the grassy lane, split by two wheel ruts cut through to the bare dirt. All the home stock lined the fence off to the left, as if spectators at a ball game. Whinnies and tossing heads greeted her next whistle.

Down at the far end, old gray Dan'l, the retired thoroughbred who'd taught her much of her racing skills, stamped and whinnied repeatedly. He'd been her friend long before Spitfire was foaled. Dan'l was the first thoroughbred her father had bought at a claiming race, back when he only trained for other owners. Right now Dan'l was letting the world know that he for one was glad she was home.

Trish gave out carrot treats down the line, taking an extra moment with Miss Tee and Double Diamond, the two yearlings. "Hey, that's enough." Trish grabbed Miss Tee's halter after the filly gave the young colt a nip on the shoulder. "I gave you both some, you know. You don't have to be piggy." The filly's nostrils flared and she tried to jerk her head away.

Double Diamond sidled right back up to the fence and reached over, sniffing Trish's shoulder and checking out her pockets.

"Think you're pretty smart, don't you?" Trish dug out a carrot for him with one hand, keeping the other on Miss Tee's halter. "Hope you remember your lessons as much as you do where the treats come from." She gave them each a last pat and worked her way down through the broodmares to Dan'l.

"How ya doin', old man?" He snuffled his way up her arm and checked out her hair, her shoulder, and her pocket. A silent nicker rippled his nostrils, then he dropped his head so she could reach his ears more easily. When she turned so he could rest his head over her shoulder, he sighed in contentment. Only he and Spitfire had adopted this position as their own. Trish gave him another hunk of carrot and rubbed his ear and down his cheek. Caesar sat at her feet, nose raised, sniffing the evening breeze. A pheasant rooster called from the brush at the edge of the woods.

Trish felt the peace of the evening seep into her heart and spirit. A narrow band of gold broke through and tinted the overcast on the western horizon. The pheasant called again. Dan'l stamped a front foot and bobbed his head, encouraging her to keep stroking him.

The sound of a car in the drive sent Caesar barking up the lane. "Gotta get you guys some feed." She stepped away from the fence and horse and started to trot up the lane. Within two strides, she thought the better of it and walked fast. She had a lot to do, including studying for tomorrow's government exam. At least she was getting the hardest one out of the way first.

That evening Marge had left for a meeting at church. When the phone rang, Trish shoved back her desk chair and crossed the hall to her mother's bedroom extension to answer it.

"Runnin' On Farm."

A silence met her ear. "Hi, this is Trish."

A sinister chuckle sent shivers racing up and down her spine. A scratchy voice she'd hoped never to hear again said, "Welcome home. I'll be seeing you."

The line clicked dead.

CHAPTER SEVEN

Trish didn't wait for the dial tone. The receiver clattered into the plastic stand. Her heart did triple time.

The phone rang again. She stared at it as if it were a rattler, buzzing its tail. Second ring, third. She reached out her hand, sure the thing would bite. She lifted the receiver to her ear. "Runnin' On Farm." She could barely get the words past the cotton filling her mouth.

"Trish, is that you?" Rhonda asked. "You sound awful."

Trish could hardly hear over the pounding of her heart. "He called," she croaked.

"Who ca—oh no, not The Jerk?"

Trish curled herself into a ball in the middle of her mother's bed. "I—I have to call Amy. C-c-can you come over?"

"Sure. I'll be right there."

As soon as she had the dial tone, Trish punched in the numbers for Amy's home. An answering machine suggested she leave a message. Trish stuttered and stammered her way through a message and hung up. Where was Amy? Where had that creep called from? Was he near? What if he had a car phone and was right down the road?

73

"God, I'm so scared!" She clutched her arms around her knees. "Help me, please." Trish huddled for a few more minutes, practicing her deep breathing to relax. For a change she was glad for the ache in her ribs. The pain made her think of something besides The Jerk lurking out there somewhere to get her. When her heart had settled back somewhere near its proper place, she let her hands, arms, and shoulders relax. "Thank you, Father. This feels much better."

She pushed herself to her feet and headed back for her room. One thing she could do—close all the drapes. If he *was* out there, at least he couldn't see in and she didn't have to feel as if eyes were staring in at her. When the drapes were closed, she crossed the room to the door. The soft light from the lamp on her desk shone like a laser on the 3×5 cards tacked to her wall. Bible verses, mostly handwritten by her father, lined the area. One in particular seemed to be lit by a flashing strobe: "Lo, I am with you always."

"Thanks, Dad, for the verses and thank our heavenly Father for me too. You seem to be a bit closer to Him right now than I am."

She chewed on her lip on the way down the hall. Was her father really closer? Physically maybe, but Jesus had promised to live right in her heart. "Huh! Can't get much closer than that." Without drawing the living room drapes, she went to the back door.

"Hey, fella," she said to the dog lying on his rug by the window. "You want to come in?"

Caesar never needed a second invitation. He leaped through the opening in one bound, his tail wagging his entire body. Caesar glued to her side, Trish crossed the kitchen to the phone and dialed Officer Parks' number.

He picked it up on the first ring.

"What's wrong, Trish?" he interrupted her greeting.

"He—he called again."

"When?"

"Just a few minutes ago." Trish looked at the clock. "Maybe ten or so."

"Who's with you?"

"Caesar. Mom's at church and Patrick went somewhere. Rhonda's on her way over."

"Did you call Amy?"

"She—she had her answering machine on." Trish could see headlights coming up the drive. "Rhonda's here."

"I'll be right out. I'm bringing one of those new phones, the ones that show the number that last called on a screen. We may get him this way. Don't answer the phone again. Let your machine pick it up and then you can hear who's calling. That way you can screen your calls. I'm on my way."

She met Rhonda at the door. "Trish, you didn't even have the door locked."

"I—we never lock the doors. You know that. You don't either."

"Yeah, but no one's threatening me." She dumped her book bag on the sofa. "I got a paper to write by tomorrow. Is Amy coming out?"

"No, Parks, for whatever good it does." Trish left for the kitchen and returned with two cans of Diet Coke. "I don't think they have anything on this dude yet and let me tell you . . ." She handed a can to Rhonda who had flopped on the sofa. ". . . I'm getting sick of it all, real sick." She could feel that she was getting mad. It always started in her gut. But at least mad felt better than scared to death.

"What do you think he wants?"

"Got me. Make me crazy, I guess." Trish stopped her pacing to drop down on the raised hearth. Caesar sat down beside her and put one snowy front paw up on her knee. She rubbed behind his ears with one hand, leaving the other free to hold her Coke.

"They questioned all of us while you were gone." Rhonda dug in her backpack and pulled out a spiral notebook. "I just can't believe it's someone from Prairie. We've known each other all our lives."

"Me neither. I bet I don't even know this—this person, if you could give him such a compliment." Caesar got to his feet and crossed to the door, a low rumble in his throat. At the same time, they could see light beams from an approaching car. Caesar set up a crescendo of barks.

"Must be Parks. Caesar doesn't bark more than once for Mom or Patrick." Trish crossed the room and let him out. The collie bounded down the walk, barking all the while. He stopped. His tail began wagging as soon as Parks stepped from his car and greeted him.

Trish held open the door.

"Trish, for crying out loud, get out of the doorway," Parks said after only a perfunctory greeting. "You make a perfect target that way."

"But—but I knew it was you." She stepped back to let the tall, tired-looking detective in.

"No you didn't. Not at first. You should have let Caesar out the back door so no one would see you in the light like that. The creep knows you're home. He just called."

"Oh." Trish felt like a little kid who'd just been scolded for playing in the street. She hugged herself with both arms.

Parks turned toward the kitchen and placed a caller ID phone on the counter. He plugged it in and showed her how to use it. "Now, tell me everything that happened." He took his worn black notebook out of his inside jacket pocket.

While Trish detailed the call, Parks sat on the hearth, long legs bent to form a desk. He tapped the end of his pen against his teeth when she was finished. "Did you hear any background noises, music, loud voices, some such?"

Trish shook her head. "He always sounds raspy, like he's trying to disguise his voice."

"Are you sure it's a male voice?"

Trish shook her head again. "But I *think* so. Besides, girls don't do this kind of thing."

"Don't kid yourself. They do, but it's not as common." He wrote himself another note. "Now remember, screen your calls and call me with the number if he calls again. Maybe this time we'll get lucky."

———

By Friday Trish felt as if she'd been to the moon and back—on foot. She dragged herself into the house after making up her last midterm exam and collapsed on the sofa.

"Bad, huh?" Marge hung up the phone and joined her daughter in the living room.

"Worse than that." Trish closed her eyes. "And to think that quarter finals are only two weeks away. I have a term paper to write and another short paper, besides one Haiku. You ever write poetry?"

"Sure, but not since college." Marge leaned a shoulder against the edge of the wall. "You want something to eat? I baked brownies."

"Do horses whinny?"

"I think that's 'Do ducks have lips?' but I've never understood that particular phrase. Brad's down at the barn. I just came up to make some calls. You want to call him? I'm sure he could use a goodie break."

"Have you ever heard of Brad turning down brownies?" Trish shook her head at the absurdity of the idea. "Or any other cookie for that matter?" She shoved herself vertical. "We should send David another goodie box."

"I know. I thought maybe Sunday afternoon Rhonda would help us. Go call Brad now."

"Let's send one to Red too. He's always giving me presents and I never get one for him." Trish could feel her energy coming back. She stepped out the front door and yelled, "Brad!"

She heard her mother from inside. "I could have done that. Go down to the barn and get him. They got in a load of hay today."

Well, at least four days since Jerk Face called. She'd made up a new name for him during the wait. Each day Marge had shaken her head at Trish's question and each night she'd gone to bed using "no call" as one of her *thank-you*'s during her prayers.

She whistled once just to set the lineup to whinnying. "Hey, Brad. Brownies are ready."

"Back here." She found him in the hayloft, moving hay that had been stacked on the straw side of the barn. When she stuck her head up through the entrance, she watched him dump the last bale in place. "You'd think they could figure out what went where, wouldn't you?" He wiped the sweat from his brow and stuck his leather gloves in a rear pocket. "We're about due for a load of straw too. Patrick said we should start keeping the broodmares inside at night pretty soon."

"We'll have to keep Firefly in too as soon as she arrives." Trish backed down the ladder so he could come down. "Sorry I can't help."

"Yeah, right." He snagged his jacket off the gate of a stall. "I know how much you love tossing bales, even when you're all in one piece." He patted her on the head, then jerked her braid. "There *are* advantages in staying small, not having to sling hay being one of them."

Arm in arm they sauntered out of the barn and up the rise. "I seem to remember Rhonda and me moving our share, even though we did it as a team."

"You're right." Brad ushered her in the door in front of him. "And as the football team knows, there's no better way to get in shape than tossing those suckers around."

Trish felt a tide of confusion wash over her. Since when had Brad started treating her like a girl? They'd always raced to see who hit the door and then the cookie plate first. She shrugged. Maybe this growing up wasn't so bad after all.

The phone rang while they sat around the big oak kitchen table. Trish rose to get it but slowed at her mother's reminding look. First they had to wait to see who it was.

A familiar voice came on. She clapped her hands over her ears so she couldn't hear—but then let them drift down to her side in morbid fascination. She felt the cold begin at her toes and work its way up.

"I'm sorry you can't come to the phone right now, Trish, but I'll call back later. You can count on it."

Trish dashed to the phone. Sure enough, there was a number right across the screen. Beginning with the 503 area code made it Oregon.

Trish grabbed a pencil out of the cup. She dropped it. Got another. Her hand was shaking so badly she broke the lead. After a deep breath, she picked up a pen and wrote the number down, then dialed Officer Parks. A ripple ran from her head to her fingertips. Would this be the breakthrough they needed? It *had* to be.

CHAPTER EIGHT

Trish waited by the phone for Parks to call back.

Brad hovered beside her, nibbling on the brownie clenched in his hand. "It'll probably take a while." He, too, jumped when the phone rang.

Trish left it until she heard the detective's voice on the machine, then picked up the receiver. "What'd you find out?"

"Bad news, or rather no news, Trish. He called from a pay phone located over by Lloyd's Center. We had a squad car out in that sector so they swung by. No one around."

Trish felt as if someone had just let out all her air, leaving her flat and wobbly, a balloon lying inert on the floor. "Oh." She'd had such high hopes. Now they were back to square one. When would they catch him?

"What is it?" Marge cupped her coffee mug in her hands.

Trish shook her head and covered the mouthpiece. "Pay phone." She took up her conversation with Parks again. "So we just keep on like before?"

"Don't panic, Trish. We're going to find him. He'll get cocky and make a mistake. I know he will."

As Trish hung up she wondered if Parks had been trying to convince her—or himself.

The next morning at the track, Trish was greeted like returning royalty by everyone, from the bug boys and the jockeys giving their morning charges a good workout to the kids cleaning stalls. Trainers shouted greetings, and every time she returned to the barn, more people came by to shake hands and welcome her back.

"Can't get nothin' done, this way." Patrick went about checking the horses, all the while grumbling around the half-smile on his rounded face.

Trish figured that today he looked more like a leprechaun than ever. "Would you rather I stayed home?" she asked, a grin tugging at the corners of her mouth no matter how hard she tried to sound serious. "Maybe Genie Stokes is a better rider."

"Leastways she don't have half the track hanging around, swapping lies and such." He gave her a boost up on her waiting mount.

Trish grinned down at the old trainer her father had hired after he'd become so sick he couldn't do it himself. "Patrick O'Hern, if someone didn't know you and heard you talking like that, they'd think you're an old grouch."

"I heard him and I know he's an old grouch." Genie Stokes, who always rode for Runnin' On Farm when Trish wasn't available, came striding up the walkway, sidestepping buckets and blankets as she came. "Welcome home, Trish. You're looking good for scaring us all half to death."

Trish leaned over and grabbed her friend's hand. "Feeling plenty better, let me tell you. But then you know what busted ribs are like."

"At least I didn't try dying on the doctors while they patched me up." She patted the horse's shoulder and looked up at Trish with a wobbly smile. "I'll tell you, there were a lot of prayers sent up from around here." She squeezed Trish's hand another time. "You take good care of my horses, you hear?" She turned to Patrick. "See she stays out of trouble now."

Patrick shook his head. "Takes the Almighty himself to do that, or leastways He bails her out again."

"Well, while you two figure out my life for me, think I'll take this old boy out on the track." Trish touched a finger to her helmet. "See ya."

Trish huddled into her down jacket, grateful she'd worn her long johns. Even when it wasn't raining, the wind blowing off the Columbia River managed to penetrate down to the bones. The gray overcast hung low enough to blur the top of the glass-enclosed grandstands. The thought of winter racing in Florida was sounding better and better.

During the change of mounts she took a moment to blow her dripping nose and drink half a cup of hot chocolate. Feeling somewhat warmer, she left the office to find Patrick holding Gatesby's head while Brad finished the saddling.

"I see you haven't broken him of his favorite habit." Trish stayed just out of mouth range.

Brad glared at her from under the bill of his baseball hat. "Anytime you want to try . . ."

Trish copied Patrick's hold on the steel D-ring bit and rubbed Gatesby's black ears. "Stubborn old boy, aren'tcha?" The gelding leaned into her ministering fingers. "Who's his latest victim?"

Brad cupped his hands to give her a knee up. "Need you ask?"

Trish buckled the chin strap of her helmet and gathered her reins. One never took a chance with Gatesby. He'd dumped her more than once. "Okay, joker, let's go see what we can do." As usual, he wanted to go at his own pace—fast. However, Patrick had scheduled him for a slow gallop—two times around the track, after a warming up half-lap. By the time they returned to the barn, Trish's side had set up a complaint department.

"I'm ready for breakfast anytime you are—and since this is my first day back, I'll even buy." Trish stripped her saddle off the now-docile gelding and walked past him to put it away. "Owww." She dumped her saddle on the trunk in the office and rubbed her shoulder. "You let him do that on purpose." She glared at Brad, who wore the same sheepish "gotcha" expression as Gatesby. "See if I buy *your* breakfast." She grabbed Gatesby's halter. "And you know there's always the glue factory for horses like you." Gatesby rubbed his head against her chest. "No, I know you're not sorry, not one bit."

While she scolded the horse, Brad started washing the gelding down. Within a few minutes they had him washed, blanketed, and snapped to the hot walker, where Gatesby followed the other three horses around the circle.

Trish hardly found time to eat with so many people coming by. Bob Diego, head of the Thoroughbred Breeders Association and one for whom Trish frequently rode, slung an arm about her shoulders.

"Welcome home, mi amiga." He dropped a kiss on the top of her head. "Good to see your shining face." He took the chair across the table from her. "What a scare you gave us! Have they found the man who has been troubling you yet?"

"You coulda gone all year without bringing that up."

Trish's heart took a sudden belly flop. "The answer is no. He called again on Friday."

Diego mumbled a few unmentionable names for the stalker.

"I call him The Jerk." Trish forked the last bit of ham into her mouth and gathered up her dishes. "Gotta run or I won't get back in time for the afternoon program. I've a term paper to research first."

"Will you be riding soon?" Diego rose to his feet when she did.

"Saturday." She glanced at Patrick. "We have one then, right?" Patrick nodded around a mouthful of pancake.

"For your amigo, too?"

"Sure 'nough. See you guys." Trish crossed the noisy room, shaking hands and answering greetings as she tried to get to the door. She'd just reached for the door handle when Emanuel Ortega stepped to her side.

"Excuse me, please," the young jockey asked, his dark eyes flashing, "but could we talk for a moment?"

"Of course, what is it?" Trish stepped out of the doorway and next to the wall.

"You know for when I hit your horses last year, I was very sorry . . ."

"I know."

"Well, the police have been questioning me about the person who is, what they say, horsing . . ."

"Harassing?"

"Yes, that is the word. I do not do that. I tell them but I think they do not believe me." He stepped closer, waving a hand to make the point. "I do not call you and send you bad letters. I want to be great jockey here in America."

Trish nodded. "I understand, but, Emanuel, the police are talking to everyone, not just you. Don't worry about it. But if you have any idea who it might be, please tell them."

"I know nothing." He shook his head again. "All I know is I do not do such a thing." He turned to leave but swung back, a smile now lighting his thin face. "Gracias, señorita. Buenos días."

"You too, hombre." She watched him cut his way across the crowded room without looking back. Had he talked with her because he really wasn't guilty or because he was? She shook her head once to clear it. *You can't think things like that!* she ordered herself. *It'll drive you nutsy.*

Curt Donovan, the sports reporter from the Portland *Oregonian*, met her at the door. "Trish, I was hoping you'd be here today or else I was coming out to see you." He gave her a hug that left no doubt about his concern. "Did you see that article by the reporter in San Mateo?"

Trish shook her head. "The one who dubbed me the Comeback Kid?"

"That's the one." Curt kept pace with her. "He says there's some company thinking of making a movie about you. Called it a 'real heartwarming story.'"

"You're kidding. He predicted the endorsement with Chrysler long before it happened too." She raised one eyebrow. "You think he's serious?"

"I'd bet on it. He seems to have better sources than I do." Curt waved to the guard at the gate, who gave Trish a thumbs-up sign. "You got a quote for me?"

"Sure. I'm glad to be home, will be riding Saturday, and don't believe everything you read in the newspapers." Trish slid into her car and grinned up at him. "And if anyone knows who's harassing me, they can call Officer Parks. He'd love to hear from them and so would I. See ya." She watched him walk back across the road to the back entrance to Portland Meadows. Rhonda was right. Curt Donovan *was* one good-looking guy.

Trish spent the morning researching her term paper at the Fort Vancouver Library, then after grabbing a burger, she headed back for Portland Meadows. Since— wonder of wonders—the sky had cleared, she pushed the button to lower the top of her convertible. What a treat, to enjoy the sun, feel the wind in her hair—except her teeth clacked together like drummer's sticks by the time she drove into the parking lot. Sun and blue sky or not, November in Oregon definitely wasn't convertible weather.

"Bet David doesn't have to worry about freezing to death down in Tucson," she muttered as she punched the button to raise the top. "Bet he's wearing shorts instead of long johns too." With the other hand she shoved the heater to high. She clamped both hands over her frozen ears and waited for the temperature to get somewhere near warm in the car. Her face and hands felt the blast of hot air long before her feet did.

"Well, my girl, you learned a good lesson there. No convertible tops down until summer, no matter how cool you want to look." She snapped down the sun visor to check in the mirror while applying lipstick. Her hair stood out all over, in spite of the braid, her cheeks looked as if someone had painted them red—bright red—and her mouth wouldn't stop jiggling long enough to put on the proper "paint," as her father had called it.

She flipped the visor back up. "And if cool was what you wanted, you sure did get that." She shoved the heater controls off and climbed from the car.

"Welcome back," called the woman at the side gate.

"Thanks. Good to be back." And it was. The sun still shone, and without the draft from a moving vehicle, Trish even thought about taking off her red jacket. The tan down vest and green wool turtleneck sweater would be warm enough.

You've been known to lose jackets that way. Sometimes Nagger could be real helpful.

So instead of veering into the women's jockey room, she headed for the track side fence where most of the trainers and many of the owners watched the races. Since it was her father's favorite place, she liked it best too.

"Hi, guys." She slipped into place between Bob Diego and his trainer. "You got one running soon?"

"Couldn't stay away, huh?" Bob moved down a bit for her to have more room. "I have one in the third. Wish you were up on her."

"Me too. But I promised Mom another week off. She gets the worries, you know."

"How is your mother?"

Trish liked the way he said his *s* softer than American-born people. "Fine, I guess." She looked up at the tall, broad-shouldered Hispanic gentleman. "Gentle man" was a good way to describe Bob Diego. And honorable. She felt proud to be his friend. "Why?"

"I just think about her sometimes. She has been through much."

"You too, my friend." The sound of the bugle floated across the track and rose above the snapping flags in the infield. The sound of it caught in her throat, as usual. That was one of the things she remembered from the day they buried her father, the bugle singing the parade to post. She lifted her chin and rubbed her lips together.

The roar of the crowd at the sight of the horses dancing onto the track drove back the pending tears.

Bob Diego laid a hand on her shoulder. "You so rarely see from this angle anymore. It is different, no?"

Trish smiled up at him. "Sure is." She glanced down at her program to see who was running and who was riding. Genie Stokes had the number one slot. Trish waved as they trotted past. "Go for it, Genie." The jockey in black and white silks touched her whip to her helmet.

A voice calling her name behind her caught Trish's attention. She turned around to drown in the most gorgeous hot fudge eyes she'd ever seen. The smiling mouth below them wasn't so bad either. "H-hi."

"Hi, yourself. Welcome back to Portland." His voice made her think of warm maple syrup.

"Do I know you?" Trish left off staring into his eyes long enough to catch a fleeting glimpse of jacket, sweater, and shirt with the look of Italy, probably by way of Nordstrom's.

"You've signed my programs a couple of times." His smile showed teeth an orthodontist would hire for an advertisement. That same smile crinkled a dimple to the left side. Wait till Rhonda heard about *this* fan. "My name is Taylor Winthrop."

"Good." Trish tried to think of something clever to say. Where was her brain when she needed it?

"I'm glad you're better."

"Thanks." Her brain finally kicked in. "Do you come to the track often?" *Wow, some conversationalist!*

"Usually on the weekends. My classes take up too much time during the week."

Classes? You're too old for high school. Trish could feel her mind working, so why didn't it give her something clever, cute, or funny to say?

"I'm a junior at the University of Portland."

College, not high school, you idiot. "That's nice." She felt like smacking herself in the forehead like they did in the movies.

"And they're off." The announcer took over and the shouting crowd made conversation impossible. Trish wished for her father's binoculars. She never needed them when she was riding and so never thought to bring them.

"Come on, Genie!"

"And it's number one by one length coming out of the turn, followed by three on the outside . . ."

Trish gripped the top rail of the fence as if she could transfer her strength to Genie. Down the backstretch and into the turn, Genie still held the lead. Out of the turn, two horses challenged her. "Go, Stokes. What're you waiting for?"

Three abreast, but Genie went to the whip and her horse stretched out, taking the lead again, stride by stride. She won by two lengths.

"She almost waited too long on that one." Bob Diego let his binoculars fall back on their cord. "You think so, Trish?"

"Yep."

"She's a friend of yours?" Taylor asked from her other side.

Trish had forgotten all about him during the excitement of the race. "Yeah, good friend. She rides for us when I can't."

"I know." He rolled his program and stuffed it into

his pocket. "Would you care to go for a drink or something? We could talk better in the clubhouse."

"Um—I—thanks anyway, but I don't think so. I—umm."

"I know. You don't know me and your mother told you never to talk to strangers. Right?" His smile crinkled his eyes. "But how can we get beyond being strangers if we don't talk?"

"He has you there." Diego turned and gave Adam an assessing look. "I need to head for the barn. See you later?"

"No, I'm going with you. Thanks for the invitation, Taylor. See you around." Trish walked off between Bob and his trainer.

"Another time, then?" Taylor called after them.

Trish turned to answer. "Maybe."

"He seems like a very nice young man. Much wealth too, I suspect." Diego held the gate open for her.

"I guess."

"Why didn't you go with him?"

Trish shrugged. "I don't know. Rhonda'll kill me for not." She thought a moment. "Guess I just don't need another man in my life about now."

Bob Diego laughed and tugged on the end of her braid. "You have much wisdom for one so young."

When Trish drove into the yard at home later that afternoon, a plain white car waited in the drive. The *E* on the license plate told Trish it was a county car even if she hadn't known Officer Parks drove one like it.

"Now what?" She grabbed her book bag and, after greeting Caesar, headed for the house.

Parks stood up when she entered. Amy occupied the other end of the sofa. Trish stared from face to face.

"All right, what's going on?"

They both looked at a vase filled with a dozen creamy peach rosebuds in the middle of the coffee table.

"Awesome. Those are beautiful." Trish crossed the room and bent over to sniff for a fragrance. "They even smell good." She stood up again. "What's the catch?"

Amy handed her the card.

Trish opened the envelope. "I'll be seeing you—soon!"

"Well, you gotta admit he has good taste." Her comment fell as flat as the silence in the room—and as her stomach felt.

CHAPTER NINE

"So the phantom strikes again." Trish collapsed on the hearth.

"Regrettably so." Parks removed his notebook from his side pocket and flipped the pages. "We called the florist. A woman ordered the flowers, paid—"

"Wait a minute," Trish interrupted, "you said 'a woman'?"

Amy and Parks both nodded. Parks continued. "I know, it doesn't make sense. She had on a stocking hat, dark glasses, and a tan wool coat. Paid cash. At least that's what the girl at the florist shop thought she remembered. It had been busy about then."

Trish looked up at her mother leaning against the corner of the wall.

"The flowers were delivered about one o'clock," Marge answered the unspoken question.

Trish stared at the arrangement. How could something so lovely bear such a cruel message? She got up and sniffed the buds again. "Well, I can throw them out or enjoy them. It's not the flowers' fault for all this, so guess I'll just love the fragrance and appreciate how beautiful they are." She rubbed her chin with her forefinger. "Shame I can't tell whoever sent them what great taste he has."

She could feel the tension lighten up by about a hundred pounds or so. "You guys need me for anything else?" At the shaking of all three heads, she grinned. "Good, 'cause I got a date to get ready for." She stopped and turned at the hall entrance. "I'm not gonna let this creep mess up my life. He can send me flowers any time he wants." She thought she heard a "Let's hope that's all he sends" as she turned into the bathroom, but she chose to ignore it.

———

Trish reminded herself later that going to dinner and a movie with Doug Ramstead was not to be confused with a *real* date. He had said they were "just friends," and she believed him—almost. But when he held her hand during the movie, the warm tingles swam right up her arm. And his shoulder next to hers felt good and solid and kinda—well, nice would do until a better word came along. When he turned his head to whisper something in her ear, the warm air set up tingles there too. Maybe Rhonda was right after all.

She shut off the thoughts and concentrated on the action on the screen. Could one be "in like" with two guys at once? She really shut that one down. Doug was her friend and Red was—Red was—clear across the country in Kentucky, even though she liked him a whole lot.

She was just about asleep that night, in the totally relaxed state where good ideas come from, when she heard Nagger clear his throat. *You could try praying for The Jerk like you did for the developer Kendall Highstreet.*

Trish startled instantly awake and sat totally upright in bed. "No way." She flopped back down. What an idea.

One of her verses floated through her mind: "Pray for those who spitefully use you . . ." This was spiteful all right. Her teeth snapped together as if her body didn't want to say these prayers any more than her mind did.

Pray for The Jerk. "Yuk!"

Your father would have. "Double yuk!" Trish crossed her arms over her chest. God sure didn't ask for easy things. She flipped over on her left side. Then her right. Looked at the clock. Nearly one.

She shut her eyes and took deep breaths. Nothing. She felt the urge and headed for the bathroom. But that didn't help either. When she crawled back in bed, she was *really* awake. Eyes wide and mind running like thoroughbreds driving for the finish line.

"All right." She threw back the covers and thumped her feet on the floor. By the time she was on her knees, hands clasped and eyes closed, she could only grumble. "Father, please bless the idiot who's sending me stuff, whoever he is." Her voice softened. "I can tell he needs you, and I know that you'll take care of him." She rested her forehead on her hands. "Please help me not hate him, and keep us all safe. Amen."

She climbed back in bed and pulled up the covers. Was it Nagger she heard clapping?

———

Thursday in government class, they were discussing—again—how ordinary people could make a difference.

"What are some things you've heard about that other people are doing?" Ms. Wainwright asked from her perch on the tall stool in front of the chalkboard.

"Our church does things like give out food baskets and stuff."

"The Salvation Army always has people ringing the bells for money. I did it once."

"People can get food at FISH. I helped collect canned goods for them one time."

"The football team cleaned up an old lady's yard one year." Doug Ramstead's voice came from right behind Trish.

"And we collected petitions for the racetrack." The answers kept coming from different parts of the room. "Helped keep it open too."

Trish nodded. Thanks to all their efforts, the Portland City Council had voted not to close Portland Meadows.

"The cub *sprouts* had a food drive not too long ago." Chuckles floated around the room at that.

"Now that it's cold outside again, I think about the homeless people who don't have warm coats or blankets." The speaker, a girl two rows over from Trish, tucked her hair back around her ear.

"Aw, they can go to shelters," a male voice answered. "They want to live on the streets."

"Right!" Trish could feel her anger starting to bubble. "What if there aren't enough shelters? You slept out in the cold and rain lately without stuff to keep you warm?"

"Naa, he doesn't even like going camping with a tent." Snickers rippled over the group.

"We could bring in food or something. If all of Prairie got together we could do a lot."

Ms. Wainwright nodded her approval.

"What if we had a coat and blanket drive?" The suggestion came from right behind Trish. Good old Doug.

"We could hand them out ourselves so we would know who got them."

"Call it 'B and C'—you know, like Blanket and Coat. If everyone in the school brought just one, we'd have . . ."

Trish heard a buzz going on—"How many kids go here?" "Would everyone bring something?" "Who cares?"

She and Rhonda grinned at each other. "This could be fun," Trish whispered. Just then the bell rang.

"To be continued tomorrow. Please come with ideas to contribute to make this work." Ms. Wainwright got to her feet. "Class dismissed. Trish, can I see you for a moment?"

Trish waited beside the teacher's desk while the woman fumbled through a stack of papers.

"Here's your test. Good job, and I'm sure glad you're back safe and sound."

"Thanks." Trish looked at her grade. A bright red *A* decorated the top of the paper. "Thank you."

"Don't thank me. You earned it."

Trish had a hard time keeping her feet on the floor. It looked as if she might have between a *B* and an *A* average in spite of being gone. Now to just get ready for finals.

By Friday afternoon the entire school was buzzing about the new project of fifth-period American Government. The B&C drive was underway with students painting signs, calling social agencies to see if their contributions were needed, and printing handouts to get the community involved.

Rhonda stayed overnight at Trish's that Friday since

she didn't have a jumping event until Sunday. After devouring two large, thick-crust supreme pizzas with the help of Brad, Marge, and Patrick, the two girls lay across Trish's bed.

"I think I'm going to explode," Rhonda groaned.

"I was fine until we made hot fudge sundaes. Somehow pepperoni and hot fudge don't mix too good." Trish propped one hand under the side of her face. "We're supposed to like, you know, study?"

Rhonda groaned again—louder.

Trish reached down and snagged Rhonda's blue book bag off the floor. "Here." She dumped it on Rhonda's stomach. "Go to it. I have to work on my term paper." The rustle of papers and the scratch of pencils were the only sounds for a while, except for the occasional groan.

"I've had it." Rhonda stuffed her notebook back in her bag an hour and a half later. "You want something to drink?" Trish shook her head. "Care if I get one?" Trish shook her head again. She nibbled on the end of her pencil, trying to think of just the right word.

When Rhonda ambled back, Diet Coke in hand, Trish looked up from her scribblings. "Where's mine?"

Rhonda stopped in midstride and gave her a you-gotta-be-kidding look. "You said you didn't want one."

Trish flipped her pencil at her friend. "You know me better than that. Would I ever turn down a Diet Coke?" Rhonda started to hand her the can. Trish pushed herself to her feet. "No, I wouldn't want to deprive my best friend of the drink she's been dying for. I'll get my own." In the best tradition of old-time actress Sarah Bernhardt, Trish laid the back of her hand to her forehead and limped out of the room.

The pillow Rhonda threw just missed Trish's back.

In bed a bit later, the room dark except for the reflection of the mercury yard light, the two lay talking.

"I have a question, O mighty man killer." Trish turned on her side so she could look over the edge of the bed at her friend lying on the blow-up mattress on the floor.

"What?"

"Can you—I—be in love with two guys at the same time?"

"What makes you think you're in love?"

"Okay, in 'like,' then?"

"Of course, you nut. That's what we're supposed to be doing now—liking all kinds of different guys, trying new things."

"But at the same time? I mean I like Red, I *really* like him. When I'm with him, I think there's nobody else. But when I'm home again and he's off on another continent . . ."

"So?"

"I felt sorta the same way the other night with Doug." Trish mumbled the words in a rush.

"Told ya he likes you."

"But does that make me a—a cheater or something?"

"I don't think so. It's not like you're going with Red or anything."

Trish flopped over on her back. "Life sure is complicated."

But it didn't feel complicated the next afternoon when she rode Diego's five-year-old into the winner's circle of the McLoughlin one-mile stakes race. Handshakes, cameras flashing, reporters asking questions— she felt fantastic. Curt Donovan gave her a thumbs-up sign and tapped his notebook.

"After the program?"

She nodded and turned to sign an extended program. Halfway to the jockey room, she heard her name being called again. When she looked past the program offered her, her gaze traveled up a leather-jacketed arm, to broad shoulders, a square jaw, and those to-die-for fudge eyes. The smile that stretched those perfectly sculpted male lips made her grin back.

"Congratulations. That was some race." Taylor Winthrop spoke in a way that made it seem as if they were the only people around, in spite of the hundreds of spectators passing by.

"Thanks. Good to see you again." Trish finished signing her name and handed the program back. Her hand touched his in the transfer. Whoa, another tingle. She snatched it back as if she'd been burned.

"I hope you mean that." His voice felt as warm as his eyes looked.

"I—ah, gotta get ready for the next race. Bye." She refused to let herself look over her shoulder to see if he was still there. Her back, however, felt branded by his gaze.

"Who was that?" Genie Stokes waited for her on the other side of the gate. "What a—there aren't words good enough to describe him."

"I know. Name's Taylor Winthrop. A student at University of Portland. Says he loves racing."

"Well, I'll sign his program any time." Genie held the door to the women's jockey room open for Trish. "He sure had the eyes for you."

"Just 'cause I won, that's all." Trish dumped her helmet on the bench and pulled off the rubber bands that kept the sleeves on her silks the right length and too snug for drafts to creep up her arms. "You up in this last one?"

Just before Trish leaped to the ground in the winner's circle again, she caught a glimpse of fudge eyes, a sexy smile, and a waving hand. She waved back and concentrated on the festivities. When she walked off afterward, talking with Curt Donovan, Taylor was nowhere in sight.

Was she glad or disappointed? Trish didn't take time to puzzle it out.

What with morning works, church, riding twice in the afternoon and trying to study, Trish found herself with her head on her desk by nine o'clock. A glance at the clock informed her, if her neck hadn't already, that she'd been sleeping for half an hour. With eyes half closed she undressed and hit the bed. Remembering the touch of Taylor's hand made her smile. Could she like three guys? *Rhonda'll have a cow.*

Tuesday after school, she returned to the teen grief group at the Methodist church. She'd attended off and on before her trip to Kentucky to get help with all the feelings caused by her father's death.

The welcome she received made her more than glad she'd taken the time. By the questions they asked, she knew the group had kept up on what was happening to her.

"Okay, let's get started." The advisor waved everyone to the chairs formed in a slipshod circle. When all were seated, she smiled at each person—a warm, welcoming smile that made Trish feel as if she hadn't really been gone at all. "Trish, how would you like to start?"

"Things have been pretty good—about thinking of my dad, I mean. Sometimes it's like, if I turn my head real quick, I'll see him standing there, smiling at me."

She could feel the burning start behind her eyes. "But he's never there." She paused. And sighed. "I guess, I'm kinda thinking about Thanksgiving—and then Christmas." Again a pause.

The advisor handed Trish a tissue. "The first holidays are the hardest. But you get through. Each day is still only twenty-four hours long."

"Yeah, but you can cry an awful lot of tears in twenty-four hours." A member across the circle leaned forward. "It's been two years since my mother died, and still I cry sometimes."

"It helps if you do something totally different than what you used to do," someone else added.

"Yeah, like don't try to keep everything the same as before—'cause it ain't." A younger boy with owly glasses tried to smile at her, but his mouth quivered.

Trish could feel her chin wobble. "Like what?"

After they tossed out a list of suggestions, she wiped her eyes again. "Thanks. I'll let you know how it goes."

"Being here every week will help, and you have my number if you feel like calling." The advisor nodded to the girl next to Trish. "Melissa, how're you doing?"

Trish left with ideas climbing on top of each other to be first. She and her mother were due for a long talk.

———

Trish approached Ms. Wainwright before class the next day. "You have a few minutes to talk after school?"

"Sure. See you then."

Trish dragged herself out of weight-training class. This was the first time she'd tried arm weights since the accident. Now she hurt—everywhere.

"How come it's so easy to get out of shape and so

hard to get back in?" She leaned her forehead against the cool of the metal locker door.

"Like it's not fair, I know." Rhonda dug through her stack of books. "Jason's taking me home, okay?"

Trish nodded. "See you in the morning."

Her face still felt flushed by the time she took a chair in front of Ms. Wainwright's desk. "I have something I'd like to add to the B&C project." She caught her bottom lip between her teeth. "If you don't mind and won't tell anyone where it came from."

Ms. Wainwright stuck her hands in the pockets of her denim skirt and leaned against the back of her chair. "What's up?"

"I was thinking—and I checked with my mother first—what if we cook and serve Thanksgiving dinner for the homeless?"

"We?"

"All of us. Mom and I—we'd like to buy the turkeys and fixings—then if all of us cooked—at a church or something over in Portland—and served it. We could give away the blankets and coats at the same time." Trish leaned forward, her elbows on her desk top. "What do you think? Would it work?"

"I don't see why not. We'll have to ask the class."

"But I don't want anyone to know we bought the groceries."

"No problem. I'll just say it's been donated." Mrs. Wainwright tipped her pencil from one end to the other. "You sure this is what you'd like to do?"

"Uh-huh. I—we need to do something different this year at our house, and maybe this way we could do some good for a lot of people."

"No maybe about it. Trish, this is a fine idea. I'll bring

it up tomorrow and we'll go from there."

The next afternoon, the government class voted their overwhelming approval. Rhonda gave Trish a questioning look and then an I-know-what-you're-doing grin.

"That means all of you have to check with your parents to see if you can help. If your folks would like to join us, they could do that too. We won't just cook and serve, we'll celebrate Thanksgiving with a huge family." The teacher posted a clipboard on the cork wallboard. "Here's the sign-up sheet. If we don't get enough from this class, we'll open it up to the rest of the school."

Trish tried to act like she always did, but still Doug and Rhonda grabbed her arms after class and marched her to a quiet corner.

"All right, when do we go shopping?" Rhonda's grin made the Cheshire Cat look like a failure in the smiling department.

"You mean . . ." Doug looked from Rhonda's grin to Trish's shrug. "Awesome. We can use my truck to haul stuff."

"Don't tell anyone, please?" Trish looked from one to the other. She checked her watch. "We're going to be late." The three charged off to their separate classes.

But that night at home, things weren't quite so smooth. David called, and as ordered, Trish didn't pick up the phone until she heard his voice on the recorder.

"What took you so long?" David sounded pushed.

"Um . . ." Trish knew she'd better tell the truth. "Officer Parks said not to answer until we knew who was calling."

"You mean that . . ." David used a name that made Trish glad her mother wasn't on the other line yet.

"Jerk?" Trish added with a smile.

"Whatever. He's called again?"

"Yep. And sent the most gorgeous roses. At least he has good taste."

"Trish, this isn't a joke."

"Yeah, but—"

"And you guys didn't tell me what was going on. I thought maybe it was all over."

Marge had picked up the phone. "If we were more concerned, we would have told you."

Trish held the phone away from her ear while David went off on a tirade. When he calmed down again, she rejoined the conversation. "I got other news for you," she said after catching him up on what happened at the track. "We're donating the food to serve the homeless for Thanksgiving. Isn't that super?"

"We're *what*?"

She could tell by the tone of his voice that David didn't think the idea was super at all.

CHAPTER TEN

"So he's not coming home for Thanksgiving?"

"I was just as shocked as you. Maybe we should have asked him before we talked with Ms. Wainwright." Marge curled her feet up under her on the sofa. "I just never dreamed he wouldn't be as excited as we are."

"I think—no, I *know* Dad would think this is a great idea." Trish snuggled back in her father's recliner.

"Yep, that's one of the hard things for me. All those years we gave what we could when we didn't have much, and now that we have plenty of money, he's not here to enjoy giving it away." Marge leaned her head back on the cushions. "I'm not looking forward to the holidays at all. Every time I think of mailing Christmas cards or putting up the tree, I see a big hole where your dad should be." She reached over and snagged a tissue out of the box by her rocking chair.

Trish huddled deeper into the recliner. Her mother's thoughts matched her own. "At least Thanksgiving will be fun. Even if David bugged out." Her words sounded brave, but inside, she could feel the yawning chasm. Would their family never be whole again?

When she woke up the next morning, an idea flashed into her mind. Trish threw back the covers and leaped from the bed. "Mom!" She charged down the hall, nearly crashing into her mother.

"What's wrong?"

"Nothing. I just had a great idea."

"Yeah, well, you scared me half to death."

Trish couldn't stop jumping up and down. "Mom, listen. What if we go to visit Gram and Gramps for Christmas? That would sure be different—Christmas in Florida. We've never been there for Christmas. What do you think?" Her words tripped over each other and came out with a whoosh.

"But who would take care of everything here?"

"Patrick and Brad. We could hire more help if they need it. We wouldn't have to be gone long, a couple of days. Beaches, warm sun, and if Gram doesn't want to cook, we'll buy dinner. You think David will like the idea?"

"We'd better check with him before I call Mother." Marge gave Trish a hug. "I think you came up with a winner this time, Tee."

Within two days, all the arrangements were made, with David agreeing it was a great idea. Marge's parents were totally floored but thrilled.

———

Trish went into finals week feeling as if someone had turned her treadmill up to racing speed when she wasn't looking. On Friday night she and Doug went out for pizza to celebrate with Rhonda and Jason.

"I have something else to cheer about." Trish held up her tall glass of Diet Coke. "The Jerk hasn't called or anything since he sent the roses. Maybe he fell off the face of the earth or something." They all clanked their glasses together.

Or maybe God is answering your prayers for him, Nagger whispered in her ear. He sure liked to say "I told you so." Trish ignored the voice and teased Jason about the basketball team. The Prairie High boys' team had never gone to the state tournament, while the girls had gone nearly every year.

"This season will be different," Jason promised. "You wait and see. With Doug guarding and me at center, we will show them all." The two guys slapped high fives. "After all, that is why I come to your school, to win at basketball."

"And here I thought you came to meet me." Rhonda pulled a sad face.

"That is how you say 'the frosting on the cookie.' " He reached over and draped a long arm across her shoulders.

"On the cake." Trish sucked on her straw.

"What?" Jason looked around. "Do they serve cake here?"

"No, Wollensvaldt. You messed up the saying again. It's 'frosting on the cake,' not a cookie." Rhonda shook her head, her red hair flying and her grin making them all laugh.

"Oh. I will learn." He wagged a long, bony finger at all of them. "But you watch. Prairie will go to state."

How will I find time to go to the games? Trish thought, stirring her drink with her straw. *Doug's already talking about me being there, like it's important to him. Men sure can complicate your life.*

She thought of that again on Saturday when Rob Garcia, one of the apprentice jockeys, cut her off in the third race, nearly causing an accident.

"Dumb punk kid," she muttered to Genie Stokes when they walked back to the jockey room, neither one of them making it into the money.

"Trish, he's older than you are," Genie leaned close to say, "and been racing longer. He just wants out of apprenticeship so bad he'll do anything to win."

"Well, it didn't do him any good. He got called for recklessness. I'd hate to be near him with my car if he drives like he rides." Trish dumped her stuff on top of her bag. "I think I'll let Doctor Dan over there work on my back. I have two races to sit out." She left Genie and crossed the room to where the resident chiropractor was working over one of the other jockeys on his table.

"Sure, give me fifteen minutes," the gray-haired man replied. "Why don't you go take a hot shower to soften those muscles while you wait."

Trish did as he suggested and let the water wash away her resentment of the offending jockey.

By the time Dr. Dan was finished with her, she felt both relaxed and recharged.

She met Brad and Patrick in the spoke-wheel-shaped saddling paddock. Crowds lined the railings to watch the preparations. Gatesby wasn't happy. His laid-back ears when Trish entered the stall said it all.

"What's the matter with him?" Trish stayed out of nip range.

"Got up on the wrong side of the stall, I think." Brad held the gelding's head while Patrick adjusted the throat strap.

"Glad you've got him and not me," Genie said from the stall next to them.

"Thanks." Trish took a solid hold on the bit shank

and rubbed Gatesby up around the ears and down his cheek. "You ready to run, you silly horse?" Instead of pricking his ears forward as he usually did when Trish talked to him, Gatesby laid them back again.

"I been thinkin' mayhap I should scratch him." Patrick checked the girth and the wide white band that went over the saddle.

"It's up to you," Trish said, all the while her hands keeping up their soothing rhythm.

"Riders up." The call crackled over the sound system.

"Just watch 'im, lass." Patrick tossed her into the saddle. "And watch out for Garcia. He's riding again in this one." He smoothed a hand down the gelding's shoulder. "Don't be afraid to use the whip on Gatesby here. You got to keep his attention."

Brad and Patrick both walked her out to the pony riders, one on each side of the fractious gelding. "Watch 'im." Patrick cautioned the young woman riding a palomino. The bugle called the field of eight out onto the track, gray in the drizzle and fog.

"Have a good one, Trish," a voice called from the sidelines.

Trish looked up in time to catch a flashing smile from Taylor Winthrop. She waved back. She hadn't seen him lately. Would he ask her to go for drinks again? Would she go?

Gatesby snorted and crow-hopped, reminding her to pay attention to one thing—him.

"Watch out for him," one of the handlers reminded the others at the starting gate. "He bit me bad last time." It took three tries to get Gatesby into the starting gate. Finally two handlers got behind him and literally pushed him in.

Trish could feel the heat rising up her neck. Today even a blush felt good. "You—you—" Trish couldn't think of a name bad enough to call the horse without cussing him out. Instead, she switched from scolding him to soothing him with the singsong croon that usually worked.

Gatesby stamped his feet and switched his tail. With the gates all shut, Trish settled in for the start. Finally, Gatesby's ears pricked forward. She could feel him settle on his haunches.

The gun! The clang of the gates and they were off.

Gatesby decided he wanted the lead. He drove past the other horses as if they were still in the starting gates. With a three-length lead coming out of the first turn, Trish tightened her reins. But it was like trying to stop a freight train with a leash.

Down the backstretch and into the turn. She checked over her shoulder to see the field a furlong behind. Down the stretch she let him go. Gatesby was still picking up speed when he crossed the wire.

It was into the turn again before Gatesby paid much attention. "Fella, you can get up on the wrong side of the bed any race day if this is what you can run like. Wait 'til Anderson hears about this. Sure sorry he's away on a business trip."

"Just went along for the ride, didja?" Patrick's blue eyes twinkled up at her.

"And to think you almost scratched him." Trish stroked Gatesby's arched neck. "He coulda gone for another quarter or maybe a half mile. And I felt like using the whip was getting him in the gate. What a brat!"

Taylor was waiting for her. "Good race."

"Thanks." Trish signed a program for a man next to Taylor.

"You feel like a cup of hot chocolate?"

"I wish. I'm up in the next two. Sorry. Maybe another time?"

"You're on."

Now why did I say that? Trish shook her head. *Do I really want to get to know him? Do I need another man in my life?* She shook her head again. "Men!"

But Taylor wasn't around when she finally exited the jockey room after the last race of the day. Trish wasn't sure if she was happy or sad. Actually, all she wanted was home and a long hot bath.

Thanksgiving Day turned out to be all that Trish could hope for and more. They fed over three hundred people and sent leftovers home with their guests. The students handed out 398 coats and 602 blankets, besides another fifty-some sleeping bags.

"I've never seen so many turkeys in my life." Marge joined Trish with her friends all crashed at one of the tables.

"If I never peel a potato again it will be far too soon." Rhonda studied the bandage on one finger. "Do you realize that ten of us peeled potatoes for three hours?"

"Be glad you weren't carving the birds." Doug was stretched out flat on one of the benches. "And I thought hoisting hay bales was hard work." He laid a hand across his forehead. "Someone want to carry me out to the truck?"

"So much for big strong basketball players." Rhonda pointed at Jason, sacked out on another bench. "What a bunch of wimps." She got to her feet and took only two steps before flinching. "Let's go home before I crash too."

Christmas bore down on them like a runaway team. Finding presents for the men in Trish's life wasn't easy. All David really wanted were more shorts and T-shirts. One did *not* find shorts, tanks, and tees in Vancouver or Portland in December, so she gave him a gift certificate. She finally decided on a coffee-table book on the history of thoroughbred horse racing for Red. The pictures were stunning, so Trish bought one for Patrick, then went back for another for her and her mom. She wanted one on their coffee table too.

It took two shopping trips before she found the perfect sweater for Doug. Since they weren't really going together—only all the kids at Prairie thought so—she debated on buying him a gift at all, but then he *was* one of her good friends. Rhonda bought a similar one for Jason.

Trish and Marge spent one evening buying gifts for the family they'd adopted off the Christmas tree at church. With seven kids and the father out of work, this family was hurting badly. After buying the groceries on the list, they included another ham and a fifty-dollar gift certificate for the grocery store. Trish made stockings for each of the kids and tucked a twenty-dollar bill in the toe of each furry red gift.

When they dropped their stack off at church, the entryway was nearly full of gifts. The youth group had volunteered to deliver all the presents on Saturday.

"Wish I could help." Trish stood beside Pastor Ron, their youth minister.

"I think you already did your share." He looked over his shoulder at the monstrous pile in the corner. "Did you leave anything at the toy store?"

Trish grinned up at him. "A little. But it sure was fun. Now I know how parents must feel when they're buying dolls and stuff for their kids."

"I hate to ask this, but we have one family that wasn't adopted."

"No sweat." Trish took the slip of paper from him. "We'll take care of it." She glanced down at the paper. What did you buy for a grandfather in a wheelchair? The two grandkids he was raising would be easy.

By the time she'd finished her shopping and wrapping, Trish could hardly get into her room. Since they'd decided on no tree, she mounded the presents all up in front of the living room window. They called the UPS truck to pick up all the ones to be shipped, including those to Florida. By the time the truck left, the mound had sunk to manageable proportions.

Even though they were leaving on Sunday, Trish agreed to ride in three races on Saturday. The cold, windy day made her question her better judgment. After the second race, Taylor waved to her, greeting her like a long-lost friend.

"Hey, Trish, I've missed you." His smile lit up like the sun parting the clouds.

"Thanks." Why could she never think of anything brilliant to say to this guy?

"Since it's almost Christmas, how about joining me for a hot chocolate after you're finished? The fifth's your last, right?"

Trish nodded.

"All right. Meet you here after I change clothes." His smile warmed her clear to her frozen toes. Whyever had she waited so long to take him up on the invitation?

Winning three races that day made her float six inches above the ground anyway. And the look of envy Genie gave her made her giggle. She *was* meeting about the best-looking guy she'd ever seen.

She was still floating when she got home. Taylor was nice, she'd finally gotten over her lazy tongue, and he hadn't pressured her for a date . . . even though she could tell he wanted to.

"He's kind of old for you, isn't he?" her mother asked that evening.

"He's twenty-one. It isn't like I'm planning on marrying him or anything." Trish grinned at her mother. "I just had a cup of hot chocolate with him. No big deal."

Christmas carols on the stereo and a crackling fire filled the silence of the pine-scented room. *Will I go out with him if he asks? He won't ask. Sure he will. He had that look in his eye. Speaking of eyes, his are gorgeous!*

Trish sighed. "Mom, did you ever like more than one guy at a time?"

"Sure." Marge looked up from her knitting. "Lots of times."

"Was Dad one of them?"

"Nope. When I met him I knew it was the real thing and I never looked at another man again."

"How did you know?"

"When you meet the right man, there'll be no question in your mind." Marge laid her knitting in her lap. "Trust me, you'll know."

Trish sat back into the peace of the room with peace

in her heart. She started counting the things she could be thankful for. Her mother—they'd come a long way. Friends—both guys and girls. Her horses—soon she'd see Spitfire. Miss Tee, a beautiful home, money to do what she wanted. Even her father feeling closer than usual. She closed her eyes. And The Jerk hadn't been heard from in weeks.

The next day she came home to two dozen roses, one dozen red and the other white. The card said, "Did you think I'd forgotten you? Merry Christmas."

So much for being thankful about not hearing from him. She tossed his card in the fire. As she'd said before, he had good taste. But who was he? While she tried to joke about it, a little worm of fear dug into her mind and stayed there.

CHAPTER ELEVEN

"And you didn't call the police?"

Trish held the phone away from her ear so David's yell didn't break her eardrum. "Well, I did eventually. Listen, big brother, I will not . . . cannot—whatever—keep getting scared every time I get something from him. I called Parks and they did the usual and still nothing. At least I love roses. I don't care who sends them to me." She winced at his groan.

"We're not being careless, son." Marge's voice held all the calm of the ages. "But I guess you get immune after a while."

"And careless." David refused to back down.

Trish flinched again. That's exactly what Parks and Amy had said. "So, we'll see you tomorrow?"

"No, on Tuesday, late."

Trish wound the cord around her finger. "I thought you got done early."

"I do, but one of the professors wants me to help finish this research project. I can't turn down an opportunity like that."

"Congratulations. You must be pleased to be asked," Marge said.

Trish wished she could have said that, but all she

119

could think of was how much longer till they were all together.

"I was already working with him, we just thought this phase would be finished sooner."

When they hung up, Trish pasted a smile on her face and joined her mother back in the living room. She was happy for David—really she was.

———

"So, how'd it go?" Rhonda and Trish were sitting cross-legged in the middle of Trish's bed, knees touching, with a big bowl of popcorn in the middle. It was the night after Trish had returned from Florida.

"Super. But let me tell you, even with a tree and presents, Christmas doesn't seem like Christmas in eighty-five-degree sunny weather." Trish pulled down the neck of her T-shirt. "See, I even got a tan line." She dug out a handful of buttery corn and nibbled one piece at a time. "You'da thought our coming gave Gram and Gramps the best present ever, but their condo is so small, I wouldn't want to live there." She scrunched her eyes in thought. "Except for the pool and beaches—maybe it's worth it."

"Did you go snorkeling?"

"Yeah, but the water right there isn't real clear. We needed to drive down to the Keys for good water." She tipped her head to one side. "Or at least that's what they told us. I coulda stayed down under the water all day. I loved snorkeling. The fish, the light—you'd love it. It's a whole new world."

By the time they'd caught up on all their news, the numbers on the clock clicked over to one. Trish groaned. "And I told Patrick I'd ride in the morning. What an idiot."

"Do you have any mounts in the afternoon?"

"Of course. Four of them. Wouldn't it be awesome to win a hundred percent like I did before I left? Three up and three in the winner's circle. I liked that."

"Maybe tomorrow night the Four Musketeers can go out for pizza." Rhonda's voice kind of floated, as if she were nearly asleep.

"Sure."

"Maybe you'll see ole hot-fudge eyes." A wisp of a giggle said Rhonda still inhabited the land of the awake.

Answering took too much effort.

―――――

The remainder of Christmas vacation flew by at breakneck speed. Trish both won and lost at the track; Taylor never showed. She figured he must have gone home for Christmas. The four musketeers, together with Doug and Jason, attended the New Year's Eve lock-in for the teens at church. Having been up all night, Trish slept most of the next day. Football had never been her thing, though Brad and David could be heard hollering in front of the television.

When Trish finally wandered out of her room, she found her mother with her head in the closet and stuff flying out.

"What are you doing?"

"Cleaning closets. What does it look like?" A pair of half-worn shoes landed in the box marked "Goodwill."

"David, you ever going to wear this again?" Marge held out a leather jacket.

"Nope, too small." The jacket hit the Goodwill box too.

"Mom, is this some New Year's resolution or something?" Trish caught a tube of tennis balls. They hadn't played tennis in years, so the balls were flat. Another addition to the box.

Marge wiped her hair off her forehead with a sweep of her forearm. "No. I decided I had to do something really busy or today would drive me nuts so . . ." She waved her arm at the accumulation. "A woman in my group said this helped her, so I thought I'd try it." At the question on Trish's face, Marge nodded. "And yes, it has. I cleaned out some boxes of your father's clothes that were still in the closet. Somebody should be using his things." Marge picked up one box and put it back on the shelf. "And when I'm all done with this, I'm going to fill the bathtub and soak while I cry it all out." She handed Trish another box. "Put that one in the hall, please."

Marge scooped up a mound and stuffed it into the washing machine. "So if you kids want dinner, you either make whatever you want or order pizza." She nudged another mound with her foot. "David, you need to come sort this."

"Brad and I were just going down to do chores."

"Fine, this will take only a minute."

Trish and David swapped looks of pure astonishment. Was *this* their real mother or had some alien taken over her body during the night?

Trish joined the guys on their way down to the barn, after David had finished sorting. That seemed the safest of all her options. She had to admit, this New Year's Day was different than any other.

Having David with them at the track the next day made Trish feel as if old times hadn't disappeared forever. But when she only pulled one win out of four mounts, she accused him of jinxing her.

"Sure, blame it all on me." David tugged on her braid. "Was it my fault you let them box you in like that? And when that nag stumbled coming out of the gate—I tripped him? Come on, Tee, you can do better than that."

She did; she punched him in the shoulder. David grabbed her and rubbed the top of her head with his knuckles.

Trish wrapped both her arms around his waist and laid her cheek on his chest. "I've missed you so much."

David propped his chin on the top of her head. "Hey, it's only six months 'til your graduation. I'll be home again before the middle of May—that is, if I don't go work for Adam Finley."

Trish jerked free and studied his face. "You're kidding—right?"

"Margaret Finley bakes mighty good pies."

"Mom's cinnamon rolls are better."

"You better come home and chase away all the guys who are after her." Brad kept step with them on their way to the parking lot.

"Brad Williams, you—you." Trish gave him a dig in the ribs with her elbow. The three of them locked arms and marched out the gate. "Why? Who else likes me?" Trish stopped in the act of stepping up into the truck. Brad gave her a boost and climbed in beside her.

"That's for me to know and you to find out."

She elbowed him again. "Rat." She watched the smug look on his face. Was there *really* someone else who had a crush on her?

———

Trish had barely settled back into the school-track-study routine when Donald Shipson called to say he felt

Firefly was ready to be shipped home.

"Unless you just want to leave her here and see if she is ready for breeding later in the season."

"You think she'll be well enough?" Marge, Trish, and Patrick were all on the line.

"I'd rather wait, give her a year. Let her get strong and grow some more." Patrick gave his opinion.

"Is she limping still?" Trish had a hard time getting the picture of Firefly in a cast out of her mind.

"Somewhat. Actually, yes. She could stay here that long, you know."

"Thanks, Donald, but all things given, maybe we should ship her back here. She may never do for a broodmare; we all know that."

Trish felt her heart hit the bottom of her belly. Please let her mother be worrying for nothing. Surely the filly would recover enough. She had the fight to get well, but everyone even doubted that. "Would another surgery help?"

"I've thought of that too. How about if we have her X-rayed again and then make a decision based on what Doctor Grant says?"

The three on the Runnin' On Farm line agreed.

"Okay, then. I'll make the arrangements and let you know."

When they hung up, Trish meandered into the living room. "Sure wish she could run again. First Spitfire and now Firefly. We lost our two best entries this year."

"Hard to say you lost Spitfire, my dear. He ran himself right out of contention." Marge tapped her chin with the end of her pen. "But I know you miss them. One thing I've been trying to learn is to go ahead and grieve for the losses—that it's okay to feel sad for the things that go out of our lives."

"I know one thing that I won't feel sad about when it goes out of my life." Trish propped a hip on her mother's desk.

"The Jerk." They said it together and then slapped hands. As Trish left the room, she threw a grin over her shoulder. "You know what, Mom? You're pretty cool—for an old lady, that is." She ducked around the corner before the throw pillow could hit her.

Saturday at the track, Trish heard a familiar voice after her win in the first race of the day.

"That's the way to start the new year." Taylor leaned his elbows on the fence rail.

"Sure is. How ya doin'?" Trish realized she was happy to see his smiling face.

"Did you miss me?"

His question caught her by surprise. "Ah—umm." There went her brain, checking out again.

"I had to go home for Christmas." He leaned closer. "I have something I want to show you."

Trish waved to Genie, who was waving her toward the jockey room. "I have to go. See you later."

"I'll be waiting."

When he waited for her at the end of her last race, Trish knew she'd go up to the clubhouse where they could sit in comfortable chairs and get to know each other without all the noise around them.

"Let me go change," she said in a rush. "And then I need to talk to Curt Donovan also."

———

"Not bad." Curt checked his notes for the day. "Two

wins, two places, and a show. Should have been three wins."

"I know. But he just didn't have any kick left there at the finish."

"And the other one did. But a nose-to-nose duel like that—the spectators loved it." Curt scratched his forehead with the end of his pen. "You heard any more from San Mateo?"

Trish shook her head. "I'll let you know if I do."

"*When*, Trish, when—not if. You gotta think positive." Curt tucked his notebook in his pocket. "You better get going. Lover boy awaits."

Trish could feel the heat dye her cheeks. "Curt! You—" But her brain couldn't find words fast enough.

"Hi." Taylor fell into step with her as soon as Curt trotted off to talk to someone else.

"Sorry I took so long."

"You hungry?"

"Starved. How'd you know?"

"I always was after a game. You want to eat first or can I show you my surprise?"

Trish ignored her rumbling stomach. Agreeing to see whatever it was that made him so excited was much more polite. "Your surprise." She had to jog to keep up with his long strides.

They headed out the front entrance and across the parking lot. Off on the horizon, a line of gold still reflected up on the gray clouds. The encroaching darkness set some of the parking-lot lights flickering on. At the far northwest corner, a black Corvette was parked across two parking spaces.

"Whoa, what a set of wheels!" Trish reached to smooth a hand down the gleaming hard top.

"No, don't touch it."

She jerked back as if she'd been stung by a bee. She looked up at the man grinning at her.

"You'll set off the alarm." Taylor punched in a code on the remote in his hand. "Now you can open the door."

When Trish did as he said, the aroma of new car and leather interior met her like a fine perfume. She sniffed and grinned back at him. Now that she was close enough, she could see the Corvette wasn't really black, but a deep Bing cherry hue. The leather interior matched.

"Want to go for a spin?" He saw her hesitation. "We could eat at Janzen Beach. I'd bring you right back."

Trish glanced at her watch. "I need to call my mom first. She thinks I'm at the track."

"No problema." He pointed to the cellular phone. "The car's a Christmas present from my folks, the phone from Grandpa. Get in. I'll show you how to use it." Taylor walked around the car to open the door for Trish.

When she sat down, the seat wrapped around her, inviting her to sit back and relax. The dashboard looked like the cockpit of a jet airliner. Tape deck, CD player, car phone, the works.

"Did it take you two weeks to learn how to work everything?" Trish snapped her seat belt after puzzling the contraption out. She inhaled. "They ought to bottle the smell of a new car. I love it."

When Taylor turned the ignition, the engine roared to life and settled into a lion-sized purr. "Call your mom. Just punch the numbers here and you'll have her."

Trish did as he showed her. "Maybe I'll put one of these in my car someday. Talk about handy." She waited through the message before Marge picked up the phone.

Trish explained what she was doing and waited for her mother to say "Fine," but instead Marge hesitated. "Trish, I've never met Taylor, and you know that's our agreement before you go out with someone."

"But we're not going out." Trish bit her lip. How embarrassing! Taylor could hear every word. "Once we eat, I'll be right home."

The doubt hovered in Marge's voice. "You be careful."

Trish agreed and hung up the phone. "Sorry. I didn't think before I agreed to come with you. How about if we just go to McDonald's?"

"We can't eat in the car." Taylor put the machine into gear and eased forward. "Knowing me, I'd spill my Coke and—"

"Would be a shame to mess up anything this pretty." She smoothed a hand down the side of the seat. "What a car."

"That's why I couldn't wait to show it to you. Now, maybe you'll go out with me sometime soon. I promise to come and meet your mother first."

By the time Taylor had run through the gears on the freeway on-ramp and eased into traffic, Trish was wondering if maybe she should trade in her LeBaron. There was something magical about a Corvette.

When she told Rhonda all about it on the phone later, she could hear her friend flop back on her bed.

"Ole fudge eyes has a Corvette and wants to take you out—and you didn't say, 'Yes, yes, yes!'?"

"He *is* nice."

"Nice! Nice! You say he's nice? Compadre, you're missing something upstairs."

"Hey, remember, I like Red . . ."

"And Doug . . ."

"And I don't need another man in my life."

"You don't have to be in love with him to go out with him—and his Corvette."

"Rhonda, do you ever think of anything besides guys—and new cars?"

"Sure. But this is more fun. I been thinking about term papers and calculus equations and filling out scholarship forms. And I've been doing 'em—not just thinking about it. Some of us have to go to college next year."

Trish felt a twinge of guilt but only for an instant. "Speaking of books, I better get busy. See you tomorrow in church." Trish hung up and ambled out to the kitchen to fill a plate for studying fodder. Sometimes she wished she could call Red, but the time difference, and never knowing where he was racing, kept her from it. She could write him a letter.

An hour later she stuffed the four folded sheets of paper into an envelope. She hadn't mentioned the Corvette—and Taylor. Should she have?

"I don't know." She addressed the envelope and propped it against the lamp base. Talking on the phone was certainly much easier.

But when the phone rang a bit later, she didn't run for it. Her mother would wait until the caller's voice came on the machine before picking it up. What a hassle that was. Trish kept on reading her literature book. They were due for a quiz any time, and she was behind.

"Trish, it's for you. Officer Parks."

Trish leaped from her bed. Maybe they had finally found out something about The Jerk.

CHAPTER TWELVE

"So, Trish, I hear you're seeing someone new," Parks continued after the greetings.

"How'd you hear that?"

"Curt Donovan. He wondered if we'd checked into the background of Taylor Winthrop. Why didn't you mention this person?"

"But I only had a hot chocolate with him one time and dinner tonight. What's this 'Am I seeing him'? He wanted to show me his Christmas present, that's all."

"So what do you know about him?" Parks' voice sounded thoroughly entrenched in his official mode.

Trish took in a deep breath, willing herself to be patient. The man was only doing his job after all. "Taylor's a junior at the University of Portland, he's from southern Oregon someplace, he likes horse racing, is a frequent fan, and . . ." Trish couldn't think of anything else to say. Surely Parks didn't want to hear about deep brown laughing eyes, a dream of a Corvette, and a smile that could break a woman's heart.

"When did you first meet him?"

Trish scrunched her eyes shut to remember. "September, I guess. At Portland Meadows. At first he just asked me to sign his program. Lots of people do that."

"Is he ever with a group of friends?"

"Not that I know of."

"Do you know where he lives?"

"On campus, I guess. I think he mentioned room-mates . . ." Trish tried to think back. Funny, but he didn't usually talk about himself. "Mostly we talk about the races, you know, like the horses and jockeys and what's going on."

After they hung up, Trish stayed by the phone, lean-ing on the counter and doodling on a piece of paper. She didn't like the thought that she didn't know more about Taylor. The next time she saw him, she was determined to remedy that situation.

If Trish thought she was on a treadmill before, by February, it was more like being caught in a hurricane. Only she couldn't seem to find the eye of it for a few days' respite. Her government class voted to buy new books for the library with the money from the Thoroughbred Association. She was on the committee to decide what the senior class should give the school for the annual senior present. Racing took up the weekends. Studying seemed to take more time, not less, as she'd hoped for her last semester.

True to Jason's predictions, the basketball team had only one loss so far and was being touted as a state con-tender. Basketball fever swept Prairie with both the girls' and the guys' teams doing so well. Trish hated to miss any game, let alone a home game.

Taylor kept asking Trish for a date, and she kept put-ting him off. He didn't discourage easily, that was for sure.

Nothing had happened lately with The Jerk either.

"I think he just gave up," Trish said one night when Rhonda was sleeping over.

"I sure hope so. You talked to Amy lately?" Rhonda lay on her stomach on Trish's bed, feet in the air, keeping time to the Amy Grant tape in the tape deck.

"As in Grant or Jones?" Trish ducked her friend's fake clobber and hugged her knees to her chest. "She says the file is officially closed for lack of evidence, but that in her mind there's more to come."

"That gives you confidence, right?"

"I don't care. Just so I don't hear from him ever again." She propped her chin on her knees. "You think I should go out with Taylor? He keeps asking and I keep putting him off."

"If you don't want to, just tell him no."

"But he's so nice, and I think he's lonesome. I gave him my phone number, so he calls once in a while."

"Invite him out so your mom can meet him, and if she likes him, we'll all go to a show or something." Rhonda pulled her gum to a long thread and then folded it back into her mouth.

"Yuk, don't do that." Trish pushed her toe against Rhonda's elbow. "*We* usually means you and Jason and Doug and me."

"You know what I meant. Maybe we should make it me and Brad. Jason would blab to Doug, and his feelings might get hurt."

"Good idea. But you know, Doug and I aren't like really going together or anything."

Rhonda gave her that have-you-lost-your-marbles look. "Right."

"Well, we almost never go out alone, so I only see him

at school and when we're all together."

"And at the games."

"He's playing."

"Whatever."

Trish thought about their conversation the next afternoon while down at the barns checking on the mare that was due to foal. Did she want to go out with Taylor? Was she 'going with' Doug? How come she hadn't heard from Red for quite a while? How come her life was a whole series of questions? And none of them had easy answers?

When she offered Double Diamond a carrot piece, he nipped her hand. "Ouch! What'd you do that for?" The colt jumped back. "Men! You're nothing but trouble."

Miss Tee, in the adjoining stall, stretched her muzzle as far as possible, her silent nicker making her nostrils quiver. "Now see? She's getting sweeter every day, and you're a pain." Trish rubbed her hand on her pant leg. "That stung, you rotten horse." Miss Tee rubbed her white star against Trish's shoulder and sniffed her pockets for another treat. Gone was the stubby mane and baby fur. Miss Tee now stood at 14.2 hands and looked as gangly as any teenager. Her long winter coat showed the bright red that would sparkle in the spring, and her lighter mane laid smoothly to the right.

"You're a real beauty, you know that?" Trish stroked the filly's forelock. "You and me, we're going to be spending lots of time together, starting pretty soon. Mom's done a good job with your training and now it's my turn."

Would Miss Tee have the speed and heart of Spitfire? She looked good according to Patrick. Trish knew she couldn't give an objective opinion, but she had high hopes for her namesake. She was foaled on Trish's sixteenth birthday and was the first thoroughbred with Tricia Marie Evanston listed on the registration papers as the owner. Trish gave the filly a last pat. "Gotta run. You be good."

Trish jogged up the rise to the house. She'd invite Taylor out for a tour tomorrow afternoon, but mainly to meet her mother. If all went well, maybe they'd go out for pizza.

Trish left a message on Taylor's answering machine and hit her books. When he called back later, she cleared her throat. She wasn't used to inviting boys—men—to things. But he agreed to the invitation, sounding pleased.

She got a big thumbs-up signal from Rhonda the next afternoon after school. "Way to go, compadre. Call me when it's all over."

"You make it sound like I'm going to jump off a cliff or something."

"More like sky diving. See ya." Rhonda dashed up the steps to her house.

Chocolate-chip-cookie perfume beckoned Trish up the walk and through the door. "Smells heavenly." She followed her nose into the kitchen where Marge was just taking another pan from the oven. Trish took a still-warm cookie from the cooling rack. "You sure know how to impress a guy. I shoulda thought of this."

"You want me to tell him you baked them?" Marge raised one eyebrow.

"Nope, but thanks."

Trish had just checked the clock to make sure it was working when she heard Caesar announcing company. Trish leaned over the counter to peer out the window.

Sure enough, a sleek, dark Corvette rumbled up the drive.

Should she open the door and meet him outside? Or wait and let him knock?

Caesar's welcome yippy bark stopped. The tone deepened to a dark woof along with a growl.

Trish jerked open the front door. The sable-colored collie stood at the front end of the Corvette, growling softly.

Taylor stood still, one hand filled with flowers and the other a square box. "Hey, Trish, call off your dog."

"Caesar! Come here! What's the matter, fella?" Calling to her dog, Trish leaped down the steps and hit the walk running.

Caesar looked at her over his shoulder but kept his place. He whimpered as Trish reached for his collar.

"I'm sorry, he's never done this before. He's usually very friendly." Trish grabbed the dog by the collar and led him back to the house. "Come on in. He must not like your car. Too fancy for an old farm dog," Trish laughed.

Caesar rumbled deep in his throat. He eased his way to the front of Trish and pushed against her knee with his shoulder, as if to shove her back.

"Easy, boy. Sit." Caesar did. "Now stay."

But that he didn't do. He kept his place right by her knee as the three of them walked up to the house. He growled again when they went in the door. And woofed one more time when the door closed.

"I can't believe him, Mom. Caesar's never done anything like that before."

"I know. Sorry for the greeting." Marge took the huge bouquet of daffodils that Taylor handed her. "Why, thank you, Taylor. It's a long time since anyone brought me flowers. And daffodils, my favorites. Makes me think spring is really coming again."

"My mom likes them too." He handed her the square box.

"Godiva chocolates! Oh my. You certainly have good taste." Marge set the box on the counter and rummaged in the cupboard for a vase.

Trish watched the two like a spectator at a perform- ance. It didn't seem real somehow. None of her friends ever bought presents for a parent. But she had to admit her mother looked pleased.

"You want some chocolate chip cookies? Mom's been baking. And a Coke? Hot chocolate?"

"Or coffee?" Marge turned from filling the vase. "And thank you, Taylor, for the flowers and candy. We'll both enjoy them."

"Coffee, if you already have it made." He took the plate of cookies while Trish dug a Diet Coke out of the refrigerator. "If these taste as good as they smell, you have a friend for life."

"You want to see the home stock?" Trish asked after they'd demolished the plate of cookies.

"Sure. See where the great Spitfire grew up?" He pushed his chair back and picked up his mug. "Thanks for the goodies."

"Come back soon." Marge walked them to the door. "Trish, make sure you check on the mare. I think it's only a matter of hours."

"You want to go out for hamburgers or something— when you're done with chores, that is?" Taylor flashed her his heart-stopping smile as they neared the foaling barn. "I think I passed inspection."

"Yeah, I guess." She bit her lip. Was it that obvious? A chorus of nickers greeted them as Trish whistled.

"They sure know who you are."

"They'd better. I'm the carrot lady as far as they're concerned." Trish went down the line, introducing Taylor to each of her friends. "The young stock are over in the big barn down from the foaling stall. Come on." She flicked on the overhead light when they entered the dim interior. Miss Tee and Double Diamond set up a nickering contest, but the mare didn't show her head. Trish walked swiftly to the double-sized foaling stall. The mare lay on her side, head flat against the straw. Two small hooves peeked out from beneath her tail and withdrew only to come out farther on the next contraction.

Trish laid her arms on the top of the half-door and her chin on her crossed hands. "You ever seen a foal born before?"

"No." Taylor's voice was as soft as hers.

"Well, it won't be long." Together they watched as a slick black bundle slid into the world and separated the sack that had kept it safe for eleven months. Trish opened the stall door and slipped inside. "Easy, girl, let me give you a hand." She picked up some clean straw from the corner and wiped the mucus out of the foal's nostrils. He snorted and raised his head, a perfect star visible on his forehead and a dot of white between his nostrils.

"Meet Spitfire's baby brother." Trish continued to clean the colt with the straw. "See that bucket by the wall? Would you hand it to me?" She kept her voice gentle, much like the song she used to calm her mounts in the starting gate.

"Here." Taylor handed the bucket across the gate.

Trish set the stainless steel bucket down beside her, took out some string, and tied off the foal's umbilical cord. Then with scissors that had been dipped in disinfectant, she snipped the cord. "There you go, little fella. You're on your own now."

The mare raised her head, curling her neck around to sniff the foal. With one last contraction, she expelled the afterbirth and heaved herself to her feet. Head down, she nuzzled the foal and began licking him.

Trish pushed herself back against the wall and glanced up at Taylor. He stood with his chin on his hands, never taking his eyes from the spectacle before him.

"I've never seen anything born before." His hushed voice would do honor to a cathedral.

"Something, isn't it?" Trish crossed her wrists on her bent knees. "Makes me almost cry every time. Sometimes we have trouble, but this old girl has been at it so long, she could write the script."

The foal pushed his spindly front legs out in front of him. His head bobbed, but still he tried to stand upright.

"He's a strong one, all right." Trish checked her watch. "Not even half an hour old and he's already trying to stand." The mare continued licking her baby, making snuffling noises. "She's telling him how wonderful he is and that he's going to be the fastest horse in the world."

"Sure. You understand horse talk too?"

"That's what my dad used to say. Every baby needs to hear he's the greatest, and who better to tell him than his mother?"

"I bet that would be good."

Trish looked up at him. "You mean you never heard that?"

"I doubt it. My mother didn't think talking to her kids was important. In fact, she didn't think taking care of them was either, so she split." The words dropped like rocks into a calm pool, sending waves to shatter the reflection and crash on the shore.

"I—I'm sorry."

"No big deal. I better get going. You need anything else?"

Trish shook her head. "No, I'll take care of her. See you." She got to her feet and watched him stride out of the barn, shoulders stiff but head bowed. *What was that all about?*

CHAPTER THIRTEEN

"But why? Why won't you go out with me?"

"Taylor, I'm sorry. I just don't have time. Finals are next week and I wish I could even cancel racing for the weekend."

"But you're going to the state tournament, aren't you? I could drive you up there."

"I told you, there's a bunch of us going. We're going to share one motel room." Trish curled the cord around her finger. Right now she'd like to curl her fingers around his neck—and shake him. He just wouldn't quit.

"Look, Trish, if you don't want to go out with me, just say so. Don't make up excuses."

"All right. I don't want to go out with you." The phone clicked in her ear. "He hung up on me." She stared at the receiver as if it were to blame. "I don't believe it. He hung up on me." She dropped the receiver in the cradle and glared at it. "Of all the nerve."

When the phone rang later, Trish waited for the voice on the answering machine. As soon as she recognized Taylor's baritone, she turned to her mother. "Tell him I don't want to talk to him." At Marge's frown, Trish pleaded, "It wouldn't be a lie."

"Just don't answer. You can return the call later."

"Not on your life. *He* hung up on me." Trish headed for her bedroom and three more hours of studying—that is, *if* she got done fast. She ignored three more calls, each one sounding more contrite than the last.

The next day a bouquet of balloons, anchored by round jingle bells, waited for her just inside the front door. The card said, "Please forgive me. I didn't mean to be such an idiot. Please answer when I call." The balloons all bobbed when she socked the one that said "Sorry."

Trish picked up the phone when it rang a few minutes later. "Yes, you're forgiven," she said after the greetings. "And thanks for the balloons. You didn't have to do that."

"I know, but I don't want bad feelings between my friend and me. See you at the races."

Trish breathed a sigh of relief. Those hadn't been just excuses she'd given him. She felt like a piece of bubble gum blown to the max and about to burst any second.

Trish and Rhonda didn't stay overnight in the capital after all for the state basketball tournament. They drove up early in the morning, watched Prairie lose their first and therefore *only* game, and drove home that night.

"I didn't say we'd win state," Jason shrugged.

"I know, just that we'd go." Trish could tell both he and Doug were taking it hard. They'd had such high hopes. "But you drew the toughest team of all. What can you say?"

"See you tomorrow at Prairie," Doug grumbled.

In March the ads she and Red had made for Chrysler hit prime-time television. Trish sat studying on the living room couch when the phone rang.

"Trish, it's Rhonda," Marge called from the kitchen.
"Really, right now?"

Trish could hear the change in her mother's voice.

"Tee, turn on the TV, quick!"

Trish did as she was told and stepped back. Red's
smiling face greeted her, and then the camera zoomed
out to show both of them standing behind the hoods of
a black and a red LeBaron. Trish had seen the rushes at
the end of the shooting, but somehow it was different
standing in her own living room watching herself on TV.
And not on a sportscast.

Marge joined her. "Looks pretty good to me."

"I guess."

The phone rang again—Doug this time. And again,
Brad. Trish didn't get any more studying done that
night. The calls came in back to back with some of her
friends complaining they'd been dialing for hours, but
her line was always busy.

When Curt Donovan finally got through, he accused
her of leaving the phone off the hook.

"I did not, but right now that sounds like a pretty
good idea. I have a paper due tomorrow and I'm not getting it done."

"So, when are you going to let me start on your bi-
ography?"

"Curt, that's a dumb idea. No one would buy a book
about me."

"Trish, my love, one of the things I like about you is
your humility. You *are* famous, whether you want to believe it nor not."

Trish let her snort give him her opinion.

"You watch—there's a movie in this yet, whether for

TV or the big screen I don't know."

"Curt, you been smoking pot or something? This is crazy."

"I'm going to love saying 'I told you so.' Talk to you later."

Trish hung up the phone, shaking her head.

She got lots more phone calls, but only Taylor sent her flowers, this time red and white carnations in an arrangement with a balloon that said "Congratulations." When she called to thank him, he wasn't there.

The next night Red called from Florida, where he was racing at Hialeah. Trish felt the usual bump of excitement when she heard his voice.

"Hi, yourself," she said. "I sent you a card to your mother's house. You look mighty good on TV."

"Look who's talking. You stole the show. Bet every guy in America goes out to buy a LeBaron hoping you'll come with it."

"Red, that's crazy. One of my friends said she'd buy one if *you* came with it." She could feel her cheeks flaming. "So, how's the racing in Florida? Bet it beats freezing to death here."

"You could come on down."

"Maybe next year." They talked for half an hour, and by the end of the time, Marge was making pointed glances at her watch and the clock. Trish checked their new phone message service and sure enough, there were three calls. David was one of them.

"So, why didn't you call and tell me about my television star sister?" David sounded put out again.

Marge and Trish were both on the phone. "I left you a message," Marge answered. "Don't you ever check your machine?"

David muttered something about clobbering his roommate.

By the time they'd finished *that* conversation, Trish glared at her watch. Burning the midnight oil was getting to be a habit, one her eyes didn't think too much of.

"Anybody else calls, tell 'em I'm not home."

On Monday the prosecutor for the upcoming Kendall Highstreet trial called with the date. They were set to begin in two weeks if another postponement didn't happen.

Trish felt her stomach do a series of flip-flops. "Do I have to be one of the witnesses?"

"You're the one he's accused of shooting at. Attempted bodily harm with a deadly weapon makes this a stronger case than just extortion. We have five counts against him, and that's just on the criminal side. I'm sure there will be civil lawsuits also."

How am I gonna fit all this in? was the question dogging Trish's mind whenever she had a free moment to think—usually in the shower or driving her car.

"Look at this." Marge handed Trish the paper at breakfast the next morning. Pictures of both a man and a woman graced the middle of the page with the headline, "Developer's Wife Sues for Divorce." She was quoted as saying she didn't want any part of his criminal activities. She was taking their children somewhere safe, away from all the negative publicity.

Trish finished reading. "Serves him right."

"I thought you were praying for him."

"I am. Isn't praying for justice okay too?" Trish folded the newspaper and finished her toast. "I'll be home late. I have a committee meeting after school."

"Patrick's not feeling well. Brad may have to take

care of things at the track, so that'll leave you and me here. Pray that he gets better or you'll have to be at the track in the morning."

"What's wrong?"

"I think that cold he's been nursing has gone into his chest. Sounds like he's coughing up his guts when he starts in."

"How come you didn't tell me earlier?" The thought of coughing flashed her back to the days when her father was so ill. Fear clenched her stomach and dried her throat. "He's going to be all right, isn't he?"

"He's not as young as he likes to think he is. That's why I've ordered him to bed."

By the time Patrick was on his feet again four days later, Trish felt as if her bubble had burst and she was the gum splattered all over a face. Stringy bits and pieces everywhere and no one gathering her back together. When her quarter finals were finished, she hit the sack and slept the clock around.

"How many mounts this afternoon?" Marge asked when Trish finally staggered out to the kitchen that Saturday morning.

Trish groaned and looked at the clock. "Only two and they're late in the program. Otherwise I'da set my alarm." She sank down on a chair and rested her head in her hands. "I'd give anything to just go back to bed."

"So call your agent and have him get someone else to ride."

"Because I'm tired?"

Marge raised a hand to stop Trish before she got going. "Just a thought. You haven't only been burning the candle at both ends, you've had a fire going in the middle." Marge took Trish's hot chocolate out of the microwave. "I think we'd better hire some more help."

"Well, when you do, hire them to do my homework."

Between races, when Taylor pushed her for a date, Trish just shook her head. "Not now. Maybe next weekend. A movie with Rhonda and Brad maybe?" She watched as he switched from pleading to pleased.

"Really?"

"We'll celebrate the end of the quarter and one more to go."

"So you finally gave in." Genie Stokes waited for her.

"Yep. He's nice and I like being with him, but I've just been too busy. This school year can't get over too soon for me."

"I was like that too."

"Some of the kids are already moaning about leaving dear old Prairie. Not me." Trish held open the door to the jockey room for Genie. "Graduation can't come soon enough, far as I'm concerned."

"So we're to be your bodyguards," Brad teased when Trish told him about their coming night out.

"You know how my mom feels about me dating an older man."

"I know, us college men are—"

Trish interrupted him with a sock on the shoulder. "Not the hot stuff you think you are." She stroked Gatesby's nose, all the while keeping the other hand on his halter. "If you don't behave, I'll sic my horse on you."

Brad rolled his eyes. "Can't do any worse than he did this morning. When am I gonna learn to watch him at *all* times?"

Trish looked at the horse, his eyes drooping in contentment at her scritching his favorite places. "Hard to believe this guy's the one you're referring to."

"Right." Brad rubbed his shoulder. "And I've got the green and purple marks to prove it."

Trish wasn't quite ready when she heard the Corvette in the driveway the next Friday night. But when Caesar's tone changed from welcome to cautious, Trish threw her lipstick on the bathroom counter and headed for the door.

"Caesar, you know he's a friend. Knock it off." When the dog didn't quit barking, Trish ordered, "Caesar, down! Quiet!"

"Guess he just doesn't like me." Taylor came around the front of the car while Caesar glued his haunches to Trish's foot.

"I don't understand it. Usually only his tongue and tail are the dangerous parts. He'll either lick you to pieces or beat you with his tail." She kept a hand on the dog's head. She could feel the tension quivering in the dog's body. *What's with him lately?*

"How about if we take my car? Your backseat is pretty small."

Taylor gave her a look of pure astonishment. "We can all fit if you girls ride in the back. Otherwise, we'll meet them there."

Trish rolled her eyes. This wasn't starting out well at all. "Fine." *Men! No wonder they called it the battle of the sexes.* "Brad is over at Rhonda's. It's just up the road."

"Make sure you kick any mud off your feet before you get in back," Taylor ordered when they picked up the others.

Trish and Rhonda swapped "Oh, well" looks. They wouldn't dare mess up his fancy new car.

While Brad raved about the beauty, the sound, the smell, the power, of the Corvette, Trish and Rhonda swapped scrunched-up looks and mouthed sarcastic words. Two people crunched in the backseat of a Corvette ranked right up near the top on a list of torture techniques. At least they weren't going far.

Their dinner arrived late and cold, and the movie had enough blood in it to restock the Red Cross. When it was time to climb back in the Corvette, Trish just prayed for the evening to get over.

"But the entire mess wasn't Taylor's fault," Rhonda said the next day on the phone. "Other than insisting we take his car—and you know how thrilled Brad was."

"Don't even mention cars. How can anyone be so picky about a bit of mud on the floor?"

"It's a guy thing, for sure," Rhonda giggled.

There's something else." Trish doodled on the pad beside her. "Caesar seems uneasy around him."

"So?"

"So, why? Caesar's usually so friendly. You know that."

"Probably it's just the car. Too fancy for your farm dog's taste."

"Rhonda, be serious."

"Are you going out with him again?"

"He wants me to. Asked again at the track today, but I don't have time, so there's no worry." Trish hung up the phone and stuck her head in the refrigerator. Where, oh where was a Diet Coke when she wanted it?

———

The Highstreet trial happened right on schedule. With all the media hoopla, Trish wondered if the trial was necessary. The man had already been tried, convicted, and hung by the press.

But the morning she was to be a witness for the prosecution, she dressed with care. Breakfast was beyond possibility since her resident troupe of stomach butterflies seemed bent on wearing themselves out before noon.

As soon as they entered the courtroom, Trish looked for the man who was accused of trying to shoot her down. All she remembered seeing was the barrel of a gun pointing at her. The man behind it had been huge, but other than that, she couldn't identify him.

At the table on the left, a man sat hunched over by his attorney. While Trish recognized him from pictures she'd seen in the paper, she could still hardly equate this beaten human being with the arrogant man she remembered.

When they called her name, Trish started to rise. Marge squeezed her daughter's hand. "You can do it, honey. I'll be praying for you."

All you need to do is tell the truth. Even Nagger was a comfort at this point.

And that's what Trish did. She told what she remembered and refused to be swayed by the attorney for the defense. When she stepped down, she again caught the gaze of the man on trial. Was he trying to say he was sorry? A flash of pity ripped through Trish's mind. *Please, God, care for him.*

Amazed at what had just happened to her, Trish pushed open the gate to return to her seat. Sitting in the back row—she looked again to be sure—it *was* Taylor. What in the world was he doing at the trial of a real estate developer?

But when she asked him that the next time they

talked on the phone, he said he'd gone to watch her "do her stuff."

"Why?" Trish shook her head.

"Maybe I'll go into law. I thought this was a good chance to see our legal system in action—and you too." He chuckled. "You looked really good up there."

"Thanks, I think." Trish hung up the phone a bit later with something niggling at her.

With the Kentucky Derby only three weeks away, Trish caught herself remembering the year before. By this time they were worried if Spitfire would fly all right, if his leg could stand the strain. How she wished to have another horse to take to the Derby!

One sunny afternoon, she led the mare outside, her foal dancing beside her.

"He's just a doll." Marge stopped to chuckle when the shiny black colt leaped away from a shadow. "He's about the most curious baby I've ever seen."

"Dad would say that shows great intelligence. He's nothing if he's not gutsy." Trish led the pair through the open gate and unsnapped the lead strap. The mare immediately found a dirt patch and collapsed to the ground, rolling and scratching her back. The colt charged away, ran in a circle, and came back to watch what he obviously thought was crazy behavior.

"We need to name him, Mom." Trish propped her elbows on the fence behind her.

"I know. Nothing either Patrick or I've thought of seems to fit. We tried something with Seattle or Slew in it, but all those seem to be taken. Since he's Spitfire's full brother, I thought something along that line might work, but again nothing."

"Dad was usually the namer here." Trish sighed,

wishing for about the millionth time that he were with them. "Did you ask David?"

"Uh-huh. No help."

"What about Hal's Angel?"

"For a colt? Sounds more like a filly." Marge rested her chin on her hands on the fence. "If you say it wrong, you get Hell's Angel. You want people to think he's a biker?"

"Well, they have a lot of speed."

"Right, of every kind. Hal's Angel. I don't know."

"I'd like to name him after Dad. Let's think about it."

The last day of racing at Portland Meadows dawned cloudy but turned clear and sunny. The fans came out in force, and with a list of six mounts, Trish felt as up as Gatesby. Only *she* didn't try to bite, or rather, nip everyone in sight.

John Anderson threatened to sell his gelding, even though Gatesby had won his last three times out, including today.

And when she won five of her six starts, Trish didn't think she'd come down for a month.

"Sure wish David had been here for this," she said to her mother when they stood in the winner's circle for Sarah's Pride, the claimer they had bought the year before. "And Dad."

"Oh, I think your father knows what's going on, and he's busting his buttons with pride." Marge shook hands with the presenter and they all smiled for the flash.

"You want to invite a bunch over to celebrate?"

Trish shook her head. "I just want to crash."

"Is *this* the Trish we all know and love?" Marge

stepped back as if to make sure.

"Mother!"

"Well, don't wait up for me, then. Bob Diego and I are going out to dinner."

"You're what!" Trish nearly dropped her saddle.

"You heard me. He's invited me out for dinner to celebrate the end of the racing season here, and I accepted."

"Maybe I better invite Rhonda over. I'm not so sure I like the idea of my mother and Robert Diego."

"Trish, he's just a friend."

"Where have I heard those words before?" Trish tried to put a smile on her face. "Oh, yeah, they were mine."

On the way to school the next day, Rhonda was yakking on about Jason when she suddenly asked, "Has Doug invited you to the prom yet?"

"Well, he mentioned it but not really asked me. Why?"

" 'Cause I think you've got a problem."

Trish waited for the light to change. "Now what?" She turned to check out Rhonda's expression. Her friend wore that cat-and-canary look that meant something was cooking.

"Well, what if Taylor asks you and Doug asks you? Who will you go with?"

"I think I'll just stay home." Trish pulled into the Prairie High parking lot. "Besides, why would Taylor ask me?"

" 'Cause he said he would." Rhonda raised both her eyebrows and her shoulders. Her silly grin left Trish certain that Rhonda knew more than she was letting on.

Now what'll I do?

CHAPTER FOURTEEN

True to Rhonda's prediction, both guys asked her to the prom.

"But what am I gonna do?" Trish wailed at her mother as soon as Marge could be found. She sat in her bedroom at Hal's desk, paying bills.

"What do you want to do?"

"Go see Spitfire?" Trish perched on the edge of the bed.

"Be serious." Marge leaned back in the swivel chair.

"Well, Doug and I've gone to school together since kindergarten. He knows everyone and so do I. While Taylor won't know anyone and half the girls will love me for making Doug ask someone else. But I hate to hurt Taylor's feelings."

"Would you rather hurt Doug?"

"No-o."

"Enough said."

"Sometimes growing up isn't all fun."

"You're right there, honey. Much of the time, it's downright difficult." Marge turned back to her bookwork.

"One more problem—what am I going to wear, and when do I have time to go shopping? Next Saturday is the Kentucky Derby. I fly back there on Wednesday, returning Sunday night. The next Saturday is the prom."

"First things first. We'll find time. We always do."

Trish left the room and headed for the kitchen. Much easier to deal with a mess of this magnitude on a full stomach. Finally, sandwich finished, she dialed Taylor's number. Maybe he wouldn't be there and she could just leave the message on his answering machine. She could hear Nagger making scolding noises. Not a good idea.

The answering machine clicked in.

Rats. She waited and asked him to call her back later in the evening after chores were finished. And Doug was at baseball practice. She'd tell him tomorrow.

When Taylor called back, Trish wished she were in another country. "So, you're going to let me take you to the prom, right?"

"Sorry, but Doug had already asked me . . . well he'd sorta mentioned it, so I . . ." She stuttered to a halt and took a deep breath. "But thanks for asking." Silence filled the receiver and echoed in her ear. "Taylor?"

"I'm here. This just takes some getting used to." His voice sounded brittle, harsh—not like the smooth, warm way he usually spoke. He paused. Like a mask falling into place, his normal voice took over. "I was really looking forward to seeing you all dressed up. You'll be so beautiful."

Trish felt shivers chase each other up and down her spine.

"Well, may the better man win," Taylor went on. "How about if I get to take you out to dinner the night before? You know, a loser's consolation?"

"Okay, but . . ."

"We'll go somewhere really nice and maybe dancing

so I'll get to see you in evening clothes after all."

"But . . ." *Now I'm going to have to buy two dresses.*

"I'll see you later, then. I gotta get to work here." When he hung up, she slumped to the floor. *What have I gotten myself into?*

"So what's buggin' you?" Rhonda asked a few minutes later when Trish called to tell what had happened. "Here you get to go to the prom with the dream of Prairie High and out to some fancy restaurant with the most gorgeous guy on the planet the night before." Rhonda groaned. "I should have such problems."

"Now I have to buy two dresses, and I don't have time to go shopping for one."

"Never fear, your friend is here. I'll go shopping and bring home some for you to try on. I know your taste better than you do."

"Shoes too?"

"And accessories. You want your diamond drops for the prom, madame?"

Trish chuckled at Rhonda's idea of what a maid would sound like. "Thanks, buddy."

"No problema. I'll just get yours when I look for mine."

―――――

After a red-eye flight east, accompanied by her mother, Trish slipped back into all the ceremony of Kentucky Derby week as if she belonged there. Having been through it all once made the second time around even more fun and exciting. If only she were riding one of her own horses rather than a colt for Adam Finley.

Red was riding for BlueMist.

With whirlwind speed, the weekend disappeared in

a puff. Trish, on a filly for BlueMist took a place in the Oaks, the filly race on Friday. She won with a mount for Adam earlier in the day.

"So, you think you can beat me?" Red rode beside her in the early morning mist at Churchill Downs. They were both walking their Derby entries to loosen them up.

"Of course. I did it once; I can do it again."

"Nothing like confidence. Just think, another month and you'll be graduating."

"I'll be free. I can't wait."

That afternoon they gave each other the thumbs-up sign when their horses were filing into the starting gates. Trish stroked Sunday Delight's dark neck. While the BlueMist colt was considered the favorite, you never knew what would happen on the track. At least the sun was shining, not a downpour like the year before.

Trish jerked her thoughts back to the present. The handlers had just gated the last of the fourteen entries. Her position as number three was ideal. Red had drawn number twelve.

At the shot, the gates flew open.

Trish held her horse firm when he bobbled in the first steps. Adam had told her to hold him back, a few lengths off the pace, so he could handle the mile and a quarter. Coming out of the first turn, she and two others seemed to have the same idea. Two ran neck and neck about three lengths ahead.

Sunday ran easily, ears flicking forward and back, listening to Trish sing him around the track. Going into the turn a rider came up on the inside and bore down on the leaders. The pace quickened. Out of the turn and into the stretch. The tall white posts with golden knobs gleamed ahead.

Trish loosened her reins. With a surge, Sunday drove for the leaders. On the outside, the horse they'd been pacing, BlueMist's Rival, kept his place. Past the three who were slowing, having run themselves out too early, and down for the wire.

The horse beside her lengthened his stride. Trish went to the whip—one crack, as Adam had instructed her. Nose to nose. Whisker to whisker. "Come on, fella." Trish sang her song. Under the line—a photo finish. Had Red's horse stretched his nose out farther—been one step ahead—or had hers?

"Good race." Red raised his whip and touched the visor of his helmet.

"You too." Trish brought her mount back down to a canter and then a trot. Winning the Kentucky Derby two years in a row would be another kind of record, let alone being a woman winning it twice.

"We have the results." The announcer's voice sent a hush over the crowd. "And the winner of this year's Kentucky Derby is BlueMist's Rival, ridden by Red Holleran and . . ."

Trish could barely hear the rest over the screams of the crowd, but it didn't matter. She blew Red a kiss and walked the colt over to where Adam and José waited for her.

"Nothing to be sorry about," Adam said before she could apologize. "I've never had one that close before, so this feels mighty good. Maybe you'll take him at the Preakness."

Trish leaped to the ground. "Thanks for asking me to ride for you. It sure feels good to be here."

"There's lots more to come, lass. Now that you're finished for the year in Portland, bring your horses south and we'll keep you busy."

Trish watched the award ceremonies with a lump in her throat. That was Red up there, and if it couldn't be her, he was certainly her next choice. The Shipsons looked like waving royalty.

By the time Trish said goodbye to Spitfire and Firefly and got on her plane the next morning, having spent the night celebrating with her friends, she was ready for the time-and-space warp back to Portland.

"You think we should leave Firefly there after all?" Marge asked after they had changed planes in Chicago.

"She sure looks good—hardly a limp at all—but when I asked about racing her again, Donald shook his head. He thinks she'll be ready for breeding next winter. Now we have to decide on what stallion."

"Patrick's been mulling that around. So we leave her there?"

"Guess so." Trish settled in for a sleep. "Tell them I don't want any food."

———————

Rhonda had found one dress but not the other. "Don't worry. I said I'd take care of it and I will. Your personal shopper will not fail you."

Trish held the bodice of the glimmery gold dress up to her chest and swirled the black bouffant skirt. "Is this really me?"

"You can't wear racing silks every day, you know." Rhonda gathered Trish's hair on top of her head. "A few curls, some extra makeup, and you'll be a knockout. Doug Ramstead will positively drool when he sees you."

"You sure?" Trish felt a thrill of excitement in her middle. This reminded her of their day shopping in California. Maybe this dance would be fun after all.

The next day Marge showed Trish an article in the paper. Kendall Highstreet had tried to commit suicide. "Pray for him." Marge shook her head. "I wondered about him that day we saw him in court. Now that he's facing prison, he must feel he has nothing left."

"I will."

On Wednesday, Taylor called. "Hope you're looking forward to Friday as much as I am. I decided to rent a dinner jacket. How about that?"

Trish felt her heart ricochet off her ribs. And she didn't even have a dress yet. Could she wear the prom dress for both dates? Wasn't it too dressy for dinner? Why had she ever agreed to go out the night before anyway? Falling off a horse was easier any time. At least she'd been trained how to do that.

———

Trish heard the Corvette enter the driveway at the same moment Caesar started barking. His welcome woofs deepened to a warning.

Trish called the dog inside and scolded him, but let him out the sliding-glass door when Taylor knocked on the front door.

"Wow! Look at you." Taylor handed Trish a box with three perfect creamy rosebuds in a corsage. "You're more beautiful than I even imagined you'd be."

Trish caught her breath at the sight of his dark good looks set off by the white dinner jacket. A red tie made his smile sparkle even more than usual. "Wow, yourself." Her voice squeaked.

"See you later, Mom." Trish turned so Taylor could drape her cape around her shoulders. She ran a hand down the side of her black velvet sheath. If this was what a million dollars felt like, she'd dress up more often.

She slipped her hand in Taylor's proffered arm on their walk to the car.

"That blasted dog." Taylor's tone said more than his words.

"What?" Trish followed his gaze. "Taylor, for goodness' sake, he just peed on your tire. All male dogs do that. It washes right off."

Taylor closed the door for her and stomped around the front end of the car. Although he closed his door gently, it felt as if he had slammed it.

A shiver ran up Trish's arms, setting the fine hairs on end. *What's his problem?* "I'll wash it off when we get home if you like."

Taylor sucked in a deep breath. Trish could see him order his face to smile, and then he turned to her. "That's okay. I overreacted. Sorry."

"Sure." But Trish still wondered: his hands were shaking.

The Top of the Towers restaurant lived up to all the rumors Trish had heard. The piano playing through dinner, their table next to the huge floor-to-ceiling windows, Portland in her nighttime finery spread out at their feet, candlelight that deepened the dimple in Taylor's cheek. He did know how to make her feel special, that's for sure. Trish wiped her mouth with her napkin and laid the snowy square in her lap.

She looked up to catch Taylor staring at her, his eyes flat and vacant.

She looked away, shivering as if an icy draft had

kissed the nape of her neck. What was wrong? But when she looked back, Taylor smiled, his eyes lit again with the warm look that thrilled her. *Silly,* she scolded herself. *It must have been the light.*

"May I have this dance?" Taylor took her hand. "Or would you rather have dessert first?"

Trish looked up to where several couples swayed to the dreamy music.

Their waiter stopped at the table with a tray of goodies, most of which Trish had never seen before. "Can I tempt you with one of these tonight?" He went on to list them all, half of them made of chocolate in one delicious form or another.

Trish pointed to one called Chocolate Decadence. "I'll take that one. Even the name sounds tempting."

"What are you going to do this summer?" she asked when the silence seemed to stretch.

"Oh, probably work for my father again. He and my uncle—"

The waiter interrupted him by placing their desserts in front of them.

When Trish looked up after sampling her wedge of sinfully rich dessert, his eyes had that strange look again. She glanced at her watch. Ten-thirty. Where had the time gone?

"Taylor, I had no idea it was so late. I have to be at the track at five-thirty." She took another bite of her dessert. It was so rich it made her teeth ache. "I'm so stuffed I can't eat another bite."

Taylor pushed his plate away, his dessert only half-eaten. He waved for their check and, as soon as it came, stuffed some bills into the dark leather folder. "Shall we go, then?"

"I—I'm sorry." Trish suddenly felt like a little kid being reprimanded by an adult. It was his voice that did it. They walked out to the parking garage and waited for the valet to bring the Corvette around. Neither spoke a word.

"Thank you for a wonderful dinner." Trish leaned back against the cushy seat while Taylor navigated the streets of downtown Portland.

He didn't answer.

Trish looked at his profile, lit by the array of colors from the dash panel. A muscle jumped in his cheek. Was he so mad he was clenching his jaw? What had she done to make this happen?

They crossed the towering Fremont Bridge over the Willamette River and roared onto I–5. Trish couldn't see the speedometer, but she knew he was driving way over the speed limit.

"Taylor, is something wrong?"

He shot her a look that made her skin crawl. With one finger, he flipped the electric door locks.

Where had her charming dinner companion disappeared to?

Trish bit the inside of her cheek. The commercial "Never let 'em see you sweat" jangled through her mind.

After crossing the I–5 bridge over the Columbia River, Taylor turned left into Vancouver instead of right onto Highway 14 heading home.

"Where are we going?"

"You thought you'd get away with it, didn't you?" Venom dripped from his tone.

Trish closed her eyes. *What is going on?*

CHAPTER FIFTEEN

"What in the world are you talking about?" Her heart thundered in her ears. "Where are we going?"

"You don't need to worry. You won't be coming back."

God, help! Trish felt the bitter taste of panic coat her tongue. "Taylor!" Her voice squeaked. *Never let 'em see you sweat. What a crazy thing—crazy that's right. Taylor's gone round the bend. God, how do I deal with a crazy man?*

Knock it off, Trish ordered her mind. *Calm down. You can't think in a panic.* "Taylor?" Good, her voice sounded somewhere around normal. "This isn't making any sense. You're joking, right?"

"No joke, Miss Perfect. You remember Kendall Highstreet? The man you ruined?"

"I did n—"

He slammed his hand against the steering wheel. "You did!" The words cracked like a rifle shot. "You destroyed him, and he's my uncle. I swore I'd get you for it and now I am."

"Taylor, he's the one who—"

"You! You did it. If you'd have left well enough alone—now his life is over. No wife, no kids, no money, no business, and he's in jail. For two years."

165

Each word pounded into her as if he were hitting her instead of the steering wheel. The Corvette lurched to the side. Taylor put both hands back on the wheel.

"Taylor, I didn't mean—"

"Yes, you did." The words ricocheted off the windows of the speeding car.

Don't make him madder, Nagger whispered gently in her ear. *Be calm. You can calm him down.* Words came back to her from a PE class they'd had on self-protection. *Talk gently. Agree with him. But keep him talking.*

"I'm sorry your uncle is in such trouble."

"It's all your fault." Taylor turned and smiled at her, a grimace so full of hate that Trish shivered and wished she could melt into the seat. "But I'm taking care of you. When I'm finished, you won't hurt anyone, ever again."

"You—you must love your uncle very much."

"I was going to wait 'til after the prom, but when you decided to go with that baby Doug, I had to find another time. You almost wrecked my plans." His voice rose again. "Like you wrecked my uncle."

The Corvette swerved on the curving river road. "You'll just disappear. Maybe someday your body will be found in the river by a fisherman. Wouldn't that be nice?"

Nice? Nice! Trish stifled the urge to laugh. If she started, she might never stop. *God, where are you?*

"You know when your stupid dog got so sick?"

Trish gasped. "You? It was poison."

"Right you are. He should have died, but I only wanted to scare you some more."

"The letters? Flowers?"

"And the phone calls. It was all so easy." His face in

the shadow looked like an evil mask. "And you didn't have time for me—hah!"

The headlights cut the darkness, lighting first the trees on her side of the road, and then the grass bank between them and the river on the other. If he didn't slow down, they might both end up in the drink.

The thought of the dark waters closing over the car sent Trish into another burst of panic. Her hand crept to the door handle. But she couldn't jump out at this speed. She'd get killed in the fall.

The car lurched again and so did her stomach. Trish felt a sheet of warmth drive the icy fear away. It was as if her mind suddenly tuned to laser-beam frequency. The dashboard, each tree—everything stood out in perfect clarity, as if lit by a super spotlight.

The smell of sweat filled her nostrils, not her own but that of the man beside her. Dank and heavy. She raised her hand to her nose to shield it. Her light perfume, smelling of apple blossoms, filled her senses. A song filtered through the fragrance of spring. . . . *I will raise you up on eagle's wings, bear you on the breath of God . . .* Her song. Her verses. . . . *hold you in the palm of His hand.*

The car lurched again.

"Taylor, please slow down. I'm going to be sick," she pleaded, both hands over her mouth.

"No, you can't be. Don't you dare throw up! Not in my car." Taylor hit the brakes.

Trish flipped the lock on the door with one hand. She gagged into the other. She slipped her high heels off, ready to run.

The car slid from side to side, tires screeching like an animal in agony.

Trish made a retching sound. She leaned forward,

pretending she was about to heave all over his leather interior.

Taylor swore, each word more vicious than the last. The Corvette skidded toward a stop.

Before the complete stop, Trish unsnapped her seat belt and threw the door open. With a mighty heave she rolled out, tight in a ball so he couldn't grab her. One bounce on the pavement and she rolled to her knees. Like a distance runner exploding from the marks, she was on her feet and running. Down the asphalt. Back the way they'd come.

She could hear the car behind her, engine roaring, tires screaming, as Taylor turned the Corvette around. The horn blared.

Trish threw a look over her shoulder. He'd turned. He was coming after her. Trish dove for the edge of the road. The rush of air from the fender, the heat of the engine, told her how close he'd come.

Trish rolled again. All her years of training in how to fall stood her guard.

The taillights of the Corvette fishtailed in the dark. Headlights cut out across the river and back around.

Behind her—a canal filled with water . . . across the road—the river . . . and a steep bank with trees to hide in before the river itself. Trish ran through the alternatives while the car turned. Could she make it across the road? How deep was the waterway behind her? Crushed rock bit into the bottoms of her feet.

Above the thundering of her heart she heard a new sound. Police sirens wailing in the distance.

The Corvette roared toward her again. Too late to cross the road. The car hit the gravel on the shoulder and screeched to a stop.

Trish thought she heard "I've got a gun" from Taylor, but she wasn't sure. She swung around and hit the canal in a racing dive.

When she surfaced, red and blue flashing lights turned the scene into a carnival.

"Trish! Trish!" Amy's voice rose to a scream.

"I'm here." Trish tried to find the bottom with her feet, and when she couldn't, she swam to the bank. Feet down, she stood, water streaming down her body. Her teeth had already begun to chatter. A flashlight beam struck her full in the face.

Trish threw up her hand to protect her eyes.

"Are you all right?" Officer Parks' deep voice had never sounded so welcome.

"I'm fine." Her teeth clacked together again. The breeze sent a shiver clear through her.

Amy and Parks reached her at the same moment. He wrapped his jacket around her, turning the action into a hug.

"Did he hurt you?" Amy wrapped her arm around Trish's other side.

"N-n-no." Trish could hardly talk around her chattering teeth.

"Can you walk?" Parks' voice felt as warm as his jacket.

"I—I left my shoes in the car." Trish could feel the sting of her bleeding feet.

Parks swung her up in his arms and carried her to the squad car. "Get a blanket out of the trunk." He set her on the seat and crouched in front of her. "Thank God you're all right."

"Wh-where's T-Taylor?"

"He took off. They'll catch him."

"H-how'd you find us?" Trish let Amy wrap the blanket around her. Now that everything was all right, her mind seemed to go into reverse.

"The cellular phone in his car. It has a device that lets the area cell know his location. We tracked you by coordinates using that system."

"How'd you get him to stop?" Amy asked, her hand on Trish's knee.

"Said I was going to throw up. He has a thing about his new car."

Amy's laughter pealed forth like joyful church bells. Parks started to chuckle and Trish, never one to be left out, joined in.

"Throw up on his fancy upholstery—what an idea!" Amy could hardly talk for laughing.

On the way back to Vancouver, Trish thought to ask, "But how did you know to look for us?"

"Your mother called. Kendall Highstreet called her."

"Highstreet called my mom?"

"That's right. Seems Taylor bragged to him about how he was going to get even with you." Amy, sitting in the backseat with Trish, tucked the blanket more securely around the shivering girl.

"Highstreet called my mom?" Trish felt like a parrot.

"You know all the praying you've been doing?" Trish nodded at Amy's question. "Well, it worked. Highstreet, being brought low . . ."

"Very low," Parks added.

" . . . decided to turn his life around—you know, like ask Jesus in—and when he realized what Taylor was planning, he just couldn't let that happen."

"So he called your mother, who called us, who called the restaurant, and you'd already left."

"I'm glad you came."

"Seems like you had things pretty well under control."

"That water is awful cold." Trish could feel the warmth of the blanket, Amy's arm around her, and the full-blast heater doing its work. The shivers only ran up her muscles now, instead of shaking her entire body.

"All I can say is 'Thank you, heavenly Father.' " Amy hugged Trish again. "And thank you, my friend, for leading me to Him."

By the time they arrived at Runnin' On Farm, they'd heard from headquarters that Taylor had been arrested. He'd wrapped his Corvette around a tree in the high-speed chase, and though he was injured, it wasn't life threatening. His car was totaled.

"Guess there's some justice in this world after all," Trish mumbled as she tried to disentangle her blankets.

"You wait. I'll carry you," Parks ordered. "Silly kid. You should have gone to emergency for a once over."

"Mom can bandage my feet. Besides, they only sting now."

By the time she was bathed, bandaged, and tucked into bed, Trish could hardly keep her eyes open—until she saw the prom dress hanging on the closet door.

"How am I gonna be able to dance tonight?" she wailed.

"We'll worry about that tomorrow—or rather, later." Marge hugged her daughter one more time and whispered their old words, "God loves you and so do I."

Trish nodded. "Me too." Her eyes fluttered open. "Tell Amy and Parks thanks for me." A pause. A whisper this time. "And please call my agent. I don't think I'll make it to the track this afternoon."

"You're right, you won't. I'll call."

Trish, in a crimson robe and mortarboard with a gold tassel, stood with her partner in the line. The band struck up "Pomp and Circumstance," and the march into the Prairie High gym began. Graduation night.

Trish turned and waved at Rhonda, two couples behind Doug. Both of them waved back. Doug winked and gave her the round-fingered seal of approval.

Trish looked forward again. She and Doug had had fun at the prom after all, even though her feet were too sore to dance. She couldn't even wear the sexy heels Rhonda had bought to go with the dress, so she wore some sandals and limped a lot.

Her turn came. She and her partner each started out with their left foot as they were supposed to. The line paraded forward and she turned into the row of seats saved for them.

She kept her mind on the program only through sheer willpower. Her brain kept wanting to play back the last few weeks. Taylor had been released from the hospital into custody at the county jail. His father had refused to pay his bail and his uncle had no money left, so Taylor awaited arraignment.

Trish had learned more legal terms than she needed for a lifetime. The funny thing was, she could even pray for Taylor. She felt a grin tug at the corners of her mouth. Her song had sure helped—eagle's wings: she could use some right now. Without God's help, that night would surely have turned out differently. A shudder ran up her spine.

The speeches done, the principal began calling

names. One by one, all the seniors took their turn up the steps, shook hands with the principal, Mr. Patterson, crossed the flower-decorated stage, took their diploma, shook hands with the superintendent, smiled for the camera, started down the steps, and at the bottom flipped their tassel to the other side.

She could do that. They were on the *D*'s now.

Dry mouth attacked her. What if she stumbled?

Their row stood and walked in a line to the side of the stage. The person in front of her moved forward one step. Trish turned to look at the audience in the bleachers. Her rooting section included David, her mom, Brad, and Patrick. Four tickets—that's all they'd been allowed. If only her father were here to see her. Trish bit her lip against the *if only*'s. Her father *was* here. He wouldn't miss it.

"Tricia Marie Evanston." Head high, Trish took in a deep breath. She mounted the steps, shook hands and smiled at Mr. Patterson, and crossed the stage.

"Congratulations, Trish." The superintendent handed her the crimson folder.

"Thank you." She smiled at the camera, stepped forward, and down the stairs. *My own winner's circle.* She clenched her fist and gave a triumphant pump at her side. Then head held high, she flipped the gold tassel to the other side.

She felt like dancing. Shouting. "Look out world! Here I come." The ovation echoed off the rafters.

Turn the page for a

sneak preview

of Lauraine Snelling's

hot new series . . .

HIGH HURDLES

OLYMPIC DREAMS

Coming Summer 1995!

LAURAINE SNELLING

CHAPTER ONE

"One day—the Olympics."

Darla Jean Randall scrunched her eyes shut, crossed her fingers, and breathed her prayer all at the same time. She repeated it for good measure, then opened her green eyes and stared at the poster on the wall above her dresser. Five interlocking gold Olympic rings topped an illustration of a dark mahogany horse flying over a triple jump, its mane braided with red, white, and blue ribbons. The red-jacketed rider, in total control, rode poised over the horse's withers.

One day she would be in that picture. She, thirteen-year-old DJ Randall—well, fourteen minus twenty-one days—would hear the roar of the crowd as she and her mount triumphantly finished the cross country course. When DJ closed her eyes again, she could almost feel the horse beneath her, the thrust of its powerful haunches sending them flying easily over the jumps. She could hear the cheers of the crowd, smell and taste the victory.

DJ reluctantly pulled her attention away from her daydream and clattered down the stairs. Her best friend, Amy Yamamoto, waited at the bottom.

"What took you so long?" Amy checked her watch.

"You've got a group lesson to teach in half an hour. And you know those little kids are chomping at the bit."

"Sorry. I got sidetracked." Darla Jean, known instead as DJ since she demanded everyone call her that, hopped on one foot while she pulled on a boot. She grabbed her riding helmet off the peg by the door, clapped it on her head, and instinctively tucked her wavy blond ponytail up into it.

"You be careful now." Her grandmother's voice followed her out the door.

"Yeah, I will." DJ's answer, yelled over her shoulder, was the same every day.

The warm Pleasant Hill, California, sun lay golden over the bleached tan hills of Briones Park to the west as DJ and Amy hopped onto their ten-speed bikes and pedaled up the slope.

"How do you plan to ride in the Olympics when you don't even have a horse?" Amy renewed the discussion they had had countless times before.

"Remember when I said I wanted to ride and you said I didn't even know how?"

"I know."

"I got a job at the Academy to pay for riding lessons, and everything worked out."

"Yeah, and how many millions of stalls have we mucked out since then?"

DJ shifted down to pump up the steep hill ahead. "So now I need money to buy a horse of my own."

"You need to learn to jump first." Practical Amy, riding in front, had to yell to be heard.

"Sure would be super to be training my own horse at the same time." Labored puffs between DJ's words attested to the grade of the hill.

They crested the hill and coasted down the other side. Aluminum pipe fences surrounded the riding rings, open air stalls, and the pasture area of Briones Riding Academy, known simply as the Academy by the working students and the others who rode there. A square white sign informed the public they could take lessons there and stable their horses.

The two girls turned into the gravel drive. "Too bad your mom can't buy you a horse."

"Right." DJ shrugged. "So what else is new? She couldn't afford lessons either, but I got 'em. I can't afford to wait around for her to help."

They parked their bikes in front of the low red barn with an aluminum roof. A raked sand aisle on each side divided the four lines of stalls fifteen box stalls long. Here lived the horses stabled at the Academy by outside owners. Some of them came to ride every day, but most of the animals were cared for and exercised by academy employees.

"I've got a treat for Diablo, then I'll meet you at the office." DJ dug in her pocket for the carrot pieces she always brought for the fiery sorrel gelding and trotted down the right aisle of stalls, calling out greetings to her favorite animals as she passed. She would have needed a bucket to treat all her friends.

"Hi, big fella," DJ grinned at the excited nicker from the restless sorrel. "I brought you something." Diablo lipped the carrot off her hand, rubbing his forehead against her chest while he munched. When he slobbered on her cheek, she inhaled a strong dose of carrot perfume. "You big silly. You act so tough, but you're really a marshmallow inside."

DJ rubbed the red's ears and murmured sweet words

all the while. She was sure she couldn't love him more if he really belonged to her. She buried her nose in his thick mane and breathed deep. Nothing in the entire world smelled as good as a horse.

Amy's whistle called DJ back to reality.

"See ya later." She tickled Diablo's whiskery lip one last time and headed back to the entrance, ignoring his pleading whinny.

"Looks like James didn't show up again," Amy said when DJ joined her. "The stalls need mucking, and I was supposed to do the show grooming today."

"We'll be here all afternoon." DJ's eyes lit up. "Extra money for lessons. Maybe there'll even be some to put in my horse fund!"

"Great. And I thought we could go swimming today." Amy propped both their bikes out of the way against the wall and stuck her hands in the back pockets of her jeans. "Come on, let's get going."

Dust puffed up around their boots as they walked across to the combination tackroom and office building. DJ lifted the clipboard with her class roster off the announcements wall and waved at Bridgett Sommersby. Owner, trainer, boss, and good friend, Bridgett was working at her desk on the other side of the large square window.

Bridgett signaled DJ to wait. "Angie's mother called. Angie caught a bug and won't be here today." She checked the calendar on her wall. "You're reviewing leads, right?"

"And starting figure eights. Shame Angie's missed so much. She's the only natural rider in the group."

"I know. Too bad kids with asthma seem to catch every bug that comes around. Angie's parents have signed her up for the next series of lessons though. Say, DJ, after you're finished today, do you want to work Diablo? He needs extra attention. His owners called and said they'd be out to see him."

"Really? I thought they'd forgotten all about him. Wish I could buy him." DJ shook her head. "Why own such a super horse and then never ride him?"

"Who cares? This way you can pretend he's yours." Amy picked up a bucket full of brushes and combs. "Where do you want me to start today, Bridgett? That Quarter Horse's tail needs pulling if he's going to show. James should be here to help out. What happened to him *this* time?"

"I guess he's sick."

"Who called in his excuse, the nanny or the chauffeur?"

"Come on now, don't be catty. It's not James's fault his father has as much money as the San Francisco mint."

"Well, he isn't learning much about responsibility when he only shows up when—"

"That's enough." Bridgett didn't waste words any more than she wasted motions—or emotions for that matter. "I'll come with you, Amy, so we can make some decisions." She ushered them out and closed the door behind her. "Oh, DJ, did you check with your grandmother about the show coming up? The entry fees should be sent in tomorrow."

DJ felt the familiar catch in her stomach. She *hated* asking Gran for money. But Mom was never around to ask. She was forever traveling for her job or at one of her graduate school courses. Not that she ever had money to give anyway.

"Yeah, I know. I gotta get to my class. Talk to you

later." DJ strolled across the dusty parking lot to the front ring where two girls, ages eight and ten, stood by the gate with their horses' reins in hand.

"Okay, let's go over your gear." DJ spoke in the hearty, confident tone that helped make her a good teacher. No time now to think about money.

She carefully checked each girth, bit, and chin strap. When she had made sure the girls were wearing the required heeled boots, she swung open the gate. "Riders up."

DJ walked to the center of the deeply sanded ring and watched her charges walk their horses clockwise around its outer edge. Heads bobbing, the horses plodded along, well used to the routine. The girls sat deep in their western saddles, heels down, eyes focused ahead on the spot between their horses' ears.

"Keep your right hand on your thigh," DJ called to one of the girls. "And don't let him go to sleep on you." After checking riders and horses again, she ordered a trot.

By the time the class was finished, DJ felt sweat beads trickling down her back.

"So how's the new saddle feel, Samantha? It must fit you better—you look more comfortable."

"I like it. It's still kinda stiff in the stirrups though."

"It will be for a while. A little saddle soap will help soften them up."

DJ motioned the other girl forward. "Krissie, you did real well today. Kept him off the rail and on a steady jog like I asked."

"He's a stubborn horse, but my mom says I'm stubborn enough for three people."

"Then the two of you should do just fine. If you could

get out here to practice more, it would help."

"I know. Thanks for the lesson."

"You're welcome." DJ watched as her students headed for their stalls to put away their tack and brush down their mounts. Both owned their horses.

DJ ignored the tiny bite of jealousy she felt. *Beginning riders and they are already horse owners. What I wouldn't give*—she canceled the thought and followed her charges to the stables. Some of the academy riders' mothers waited patiently in their expensive, air-conditioned cars; others walked to the stalls to hurry their daughters along.

"DJ, when can our group go trail-riding in the Briones?" Samantha asked. Briones State Park bordered the west edge of the Academy's acreage.

"You guys have done so good! We'll pack lunches and go in two weeks. But, Sam, you need to get over here to practice more. You could be a really good rider if you did."

"I wish, but my mom is expecting a baby. She says she's too miserable to drive me over every day."

"So ride your bike."

The slender girl shook her head. "Too far. And Mom says the road's too dangerous." She scuffed her boot toe in the dust, studying the patterns she drew. "I want to be the best—you know, compete in the shows and stuff." She looked up at DJ, dark eyes serious. "Like you do."

DJ felt a curious knot in her middle. This could have been her at eight. Only her mom wouldn't have been pregnant. Of course, if her mom had ever found someone to remarry, maybe there would have been a brother or sister for—DJ slammed the lid on those thoughts. She *never* let them out when other people were around.

"If you want it bad enough, you can make it happen." She knew where the words had come from. She hadn't planned on saying such a thing. But then, she hadn't planned on having this conversation either.

DJ grinned and tweaked Sam's red ponytail. She repeated her grandmother's words again, "If you want something bad enough, you can make it happen." Of course, Gran said to pray about it too, but DJ didn't think this was the right place to bring praying up. She ought to ask Gran out here to give the girls a pep talk, like a coach before a big game.

"You better get Soda brushed down, Sam. Your mom is waiting."

DJ joked with the girls while she supervised them caring for their horses. She did the heavy work—lifting the western saddles down and standing them on their horns in the aisle—but each girl had to groom her own horse and take care of the stall and tack. While some people paid the Academy for these services, other parents felt that caring for a horse was part of ownership. DJ agreed.

She waved them both off, then walked back to the office. Maybe Bridgett had time to talk now. Horses nickered for attention when she passed their stalls. She could hear Amy talking to someone over in the other aisle. It sounded like James had finally made it to work.

But when DJ got to the office, the academy owner was busy with another client, so she returned to the barns. There were still three stalls to muck out on this aisle before she could work with Diablo. She snapped the horses on the hot walker, cleaned the stalls, and spread new shavings in record time. Maybe she'd give Diablo a bath after riding him.

DJ wiped the sweat off her face with the hem of her T-shirt. This July day was meeting its earlier promise of being warm to hot. She stopped at the drinking fountain on the north side of the stable and guzzled the tepid water before splashing some on her face. She'd make sure to splash plenty on herself while bathing the big red horse. The day was growing long. DJ wished she'd brought a lunch.

"Hi, fella, you miss me?" She stopped in front of the impatient gelding and slung her English saddle over the stall's half door. Diablo pawed the shavings down to the hard-packed dirt. He snorted, then pricked his ears forward. DJ stroked his long forelock and brushed it off the bright white diamond in the center of his forehead. A cowlick in the center swirled the hairs in a circle. "You're such a beauty. If only I could buy you. Wonder how much I'd need?"

He rubbed his forehead against her, leaving red and white hairs on her royal blue T-shirt. DJ tickled the hairs sticking out of his ears. "Let's get going, you old silly." She kept up the easy murmur she used when working with the horses, talking to the sleek Thoroughbred-Quarter Horse cross as if he understood every word— and answered. Once he was bridled and saddled, she led him out to the cement block for mounting.

Today, just for today, she would pretend Diablo really *was* hers. After all, she *would* be showing him in less than two weeks. His owners, Mr. and Mrs. Ortega, seemed to appreciate how well she and Diablo were doing in the English Pleasure and the Trail Horse classes.

DJ spent the next hour and a half taking the gelding through the entire routine for both classes. By the time they finished, both girl and horse wore a sheen of sweat.

"You two looked mighty good out there," Bridgett met them at the gate and swung it open. "You've got him in top shape, both condition and training. Sure has improved since he came in."

"Do you think the Ortegas would like him to learn to jump?"

"I'll ask. But seems to me *you* better learn first."

"I know. I want to so bad. How much would lessons cost?"

"Aren't you earning enough right now? I've just been waiting for you to ask. But you'll need to start on old Megs. She knows the bars so well, she'll be a good tutor for you."

DJ felt sure her face would split. She gave a decidedly unprofessional bounce in the saddle. Diablo threw his head up, and she tightened her grip on the reins. "Easy, boy, sorry about that. When can I start?"

Bridgett smiled up at her star pupil. "Is tomorrow at eight all right? I know that's earlier than you usually come, but let's do it before the sun gets too hot." She slapped DJ on the knee and turned to leave. "Oh, I'll ask the Ortegas tonight about jumping Diablo. You already have a good seat, so with some experience you could work with him."

DJ could almost see the Olympic rings shining on the wall of the building in front of her. She waved as Amy rode one of the stable horses into the ring. Amy preferred western riding, so the two of them usually didn't compete in the same classes.

James followed on his dapple gray Arab filly. DJ shook her head in disgust. If *she* had a horse like that, she'd sure find it easier to smile than he did.

If James had been one of her students, she would

have told him to keep his back straight, his chin up, and his heels down.

But he wasn't, and the last time she had made a suggestion—well, James had made it clear that he didn't take suggestions—or even orders—from *anyone*. When DJ told Gran about the situation, she had said James really needed a friend.

"He can find someone else," DJ muttered, turning back to the barn. She could clean tack until Amy finished her lesson. Rubbing saddle soap into the leathers of a saddle required no brain power, leaving her mind free to explore the challenges of the Olympic long course. Cross country was the most difficult. She and Diablo would jump clean all the way around with the fastest time ever clocked. *First the triple jump, then the brush, then over a creek . . .*

"You ready to go home or what?" The tone of Amy's voice indicated she'd asked the question before.

DJ jerked herself back to reality. The saddle she was soaping up had *some* shine to it.

Her pumping legs slowed when she pedaled from Amy's house to her own. Now she had to ask for money for the class entry fees. Maybe she should take it out of her horse account. But Gran had promised she would pay the entrance fees. All DJ had to do was ask.

DJ smiled. Why not require a signature in blood or a week of hard time digging in the backyard? Maybe she should offer to clean the kitchen every night without grumping. Not grumbling was the key. Even scrubbing toilets was better than doing dishes. DJ parked her bike carefully in the garage. Nothing fried her mother like something out of place.

Gran was so different from her mom. All Gran said

to do was ask. She also told DJ to ask God when she needed something. DJ did remember to ask God for the most important things—at least some of the time. Like winning Olympic gold. It just didn't seem fair to bother God with the little things. She chewed on her thumbnail as she walked through the back door.

"Gran?"

"In the studio."

DJ padded through the living room and out to her grandmother's studio. In a normal family's home, it would have been the family room. Gran, a highly successful illustrator, stood in front of her easel, brush in hand and head cocked, studying her latest work.

"What do you think?"

DJ looked from the whimsical forest creatures dancing on the canvas to her grandmother dressed in matching hot pink shorts and tank top, both liberally decorated with bright dabs of paint. "The painting is awesome, like always, and you have yellow paint on your chin."

"No biggie." The artist stepped forward and applied two more brushstrokes to the fawn, bringing his spotted coat to life. "There, I'll leave it 'til tomorrow. I actually think it's done."

DJ sank into the stuffed rocker, her feet trailing over the arm. "Gran?"

"What, my darling?" The voice sounded vague, as if Gran were still off in the forest with her creatures.

DJ drew a circle around the puckered scar on her left palm. The words wouldn't come. "When's Mom coming home?"

"Tomorrow night. Why?" Gran continued setting her paints in order. Other things might be left scattered around, but her paints and brushes were always cleaned and organized when she finished for the day.

"I need—ah—Gran, I need money for entry fees." The words stumbled over each other in their rush to reach air.

"Of course, why the hesitation? All you have to do is ask." Gran turned around, hands on her rounded hips. "How much do you need and by when?"

The whoosh leaving DJ's lungs set the folded paper swans attached to a twisted branch dancing on their threads. She named the amount.

"Check or cash?" Gran wiped the wisps of salt-and-pepper hair—heavy on the salt—back from her forehead. A puzzled look flitted across her face. "Did you have lunch? I don't think I did. What time is it anyway?" While she talked she dug in her huge, satchel-style purse and pulled out a battered billfold. She wrote and handed DJ a check.

"I'll pay you back."

"You pay me back just by being yourself and helping when I ask. Working to pay for your own lessons is a big help. Besides, when was the last time I had to take out the garbage or mow and water the yard?" She threw her arm over DJ's shoulder and squeezed. "I just thank God I have money to give you."

DJ ducked her head, suddenly shy. That was her Gran all right. Always thankful for everything. But she *would* pay her back somehow.

Right after dinner, Gran buried her head in a book.

DJ climbed the stairs to her bedroom. This was the best time of day to draw. DJ's own pictures of horses filled her walls. Charcoal or pencil foals, Arabs, and jumpers surrounded the colored Olympic poster.

She piled her pillows against the headboard, propped her drawing board on her knees, and leaned back, waiting for inspiration to strike. Her pencil began to move as if controlled by some unseen force. Later, her drawing finished, she fell asleep with horses on her mind, the main one a fiery sorrel sporting a startling white diamond in the center of his forehead.

DJ rode out to the Academy by herself in the morning. Amy would be coming later. Her whistle set all the horses nickering as she jogged down the sandy aisle toward the red gelding's stall.

But Diablo didn't answer her whistle. His stall gate stood open, hooked to the side wall. All of his gear had been cleared out. Even the shavings had been swept away, leaving nothing but bare black dirt. DJ felt her happiness escape her with a whoosh. Diablo was gone.